A Matter Of Trust

Fiona Marsden

16pt

Read How You Want

LARGE PRINT BOOKS, BRAILLE & DAISY

Copyright Page from the Original Book

ESCAPE
publishing

Title: A MATTER OF TRUST

Copyright © 2021 by Fiona Marsden

Published by
Escape
An imprint of Harlequin Enterprises (Australia) Pty Limited (ABN 47 001 180 918), a subsidiary of HarperCollins Publishers Australia Pty Limited (ABN 36 009 913 517)
Level 13, 201 Elizabeth St
SYDNEY NSW 2000
AUSTRALIA

www.romance.com.au

TABLE OF CONTENTS

INTRODUCING

ROMANCE
.COM.AU

RURAL | CONTEMPORARY | FANTASY | HISTORICAL | PARANORMAL | ROMANTIC SUSPENSE | LGBTQI

All the books you love with all the romance you need!

A Matter of Trust

Fiona Marsden

Twelve years is a long time to hide a secret ... or two.

Forced from his self-imposed exile, Doctor Morgan Cavanaugh must face his demons and confront the girl he left behind. Becca Walters became a woman in that time with life-altering revelations of her own.

Becca fought her way to respectability, but it came at a cost. With Morgan's return she must face the consequences of long-ago decisions, made without his knowledge.

Together they have to face the past; in order to make a future.

A moving contemporary romance about facing past regrets and the search for belonging from a fabulous new talent. Perfect reading for anyone who loves Mandy Magro.

About the author

FIONA MARSDEN has lived most of her life in rural Australia, sharing her five-acre block with kangaroos, wallabies and the odd koala and possum. Born and bred in Queensland, Australia, Fiona grew up in the far west of the state, lived for several years in Brisbane and is now settled on the Granite Belt in the rural south east.

Writing has always been a passion, from poetry published in *The Courier Mail* and school annuals to grant applications that require a vivid imagination, then finally finding her place writing happy endings. Fiona has been fortunate in winning and placing in a number of writing awards both here and overseas. Several stories have been published in anthologies and she has self-published several romance novels and novellas.
fionamarsden.com

Twitter and Instagram: @fionammarsden

Facebook Author Page: https://www.facebook.co m/PrincessFionaMarsden

To my family.
It's been a long and winding road.

And to the Stanthorpe Sirens.

Chapter I

Two weeks to D-day. Or M-day. Rebecca Walters glanced at the calendar on her laptop with the staff shifts colour-coded. She hadn't put a code for Doctor Morgan Cavanaugh on yet.

Her own code as practice manager blinked at her and she couldn't help wondering how long it would stay.

Would Morgan be willing to work with her?

Especially once he found out the truth about the past. She couldn't afford to go back to her old job at the nursing home. Not with the mountain of debt her parents, mainly her stepfather, had left behind. Once her mother died, it had been a relief to repossess her birth father's name, leaving Bujold in the past where it belonged.

'Becca?' The clinic nurse hovered at the door of her office behind reception. 'The pharma rep is here.'

'Thanks, Karen.' With a sigh, Becca closed the laptop. She could finish it later. Normally she loved her job, loved the challenge, but with the date of Morgan's arrival looming, it made her edgy.

The rep was easy to deal with. He flirted as usual. It was a game he played but he knew

Becca wasn't up for a night out. Not on a school night. Not with the responsibility of two children and a step-cousin with a brain injury to keep her busy. At least Dan would be moving to his own place in neighbouring Bialga with some friends soon. It would make it easier, especially for the twins.

Another problem she'd have to deal with. She couldn't use Morgan's parents for childcare once Morgan came home. Grace had made her position clear at the start when the twins were born and they'd made the deal.

Help in return for silence.

It had hurt, but not as much as believing Morgan had deliberately turned his back on his children. Lately, Grace was oddly reluctant for Becca to find alternative arrangements. After all this time, Morgan's mother had become fond of the children and they adored Grandpa Ned. Grace's cooking was the drawcard in the relationship. Sometimes Becca wondered if Grace regretted the deal as much as Becca did. Neither of them expected it to last all this time. Except Morgan never came home and things drifted into an uneasy peace.

The twins were used to their current routine and would miss the daily contact with Ned and Grace. Free or cheap childcare for two eleven-year-olds was hard to find when she had no vehicle to do pickups and drop-offs. She'd planned on buying a small second-hand car soon, but with her job no longer secure, she'd been too uncertain to make such a large financial commitment.

Frustrated at her unusual distraction, Becca glanced at her watch. Time for her meeting with Doctor Farrell. He was usually happy to leave the running of the clinic to her, with the assistance of the staff. This close to retirement, he was pretty much cruising until his replacement arrived. He at least was happy it was Morgan. He'd been Morgan's mentor during high school when he'd first shown an interest in medicine, rather than following Ned Cavanaugh in farming his family's block of land.

'All ready for the transition?'

Becca nodded, checking the to do list on her tablet. 'Prescription and pharmaceutical software is all up to date. Client database is stripped of any patients who've left and all current records were checked for accuracy. We had a few incorrect addresses but mostly it's been running properly.'

He rested his clasped hands on his ample waist. 'I'm looking forward to not having to worry about these things.'

In reality, he'd never worried. He left the technical side of things to Becca and focused on the medicine. Which suited her fine. 'You'll enjoy the warmer weather when you move down to the coast.'

'It'll be a change. I'll probably get down there and miss the cool nights.'

'Air conditioning will do the job.' She braced herself. 'Have you been in contact with Doctor Cavanaugh?'

'I spoke to him late last week. He has a few medical check-ups to complete before he leaves Brisbane. I imagine he'll want plenty of time to settle in and catch up with his parents.'

In other words, he might get here before the two weeks stated on the contract. She'd need to speak to Grace sooner rather than later about the twins. The moment he saw Gabby, he'd know the truth. She didn't want to think about how angry he'd be. She remembered his temper, though it had been rarely displayed.

Returning to her office, she mired herself in the staff shifts, clearing her head of the fears and uncertainty. She'd talk to Grace this afternoon when she picked up the children. The rest of it would have to wait. This job was vital to her children's future. She couldn't risk it. Not now.

*

Becca was tidying up, ready to lock the front door when one of the regular patients burst through the door, a bellowing youngster clutched to her chest. At the sight of blood on the child's clothes and bare legs, Becca grabbed a dressing pack from the storeroom behind the reception area and almost ran to meet them.

'You should have bandaged Craig's leg before you brought him into town, Kaylee.' Shifting her grip on the dressing pressed over the wound, Becca contemplated the simplest way to remove the sobbing child from the hysterical young mother. The woman had frozen the moment she'd made it through the door.

She glanced towards the back of the reception area. 'Karen?'

The clinic nurse poked her head out of the treatment room. 'Nearly finished.'

'Can you come as soon as you're done? We'll also need Bert to clean up ASAP.'

Carefully Rebecca eased the shaking woman down onto one of the chairs in the waiting room. Kaylee was a good mother, despite her youth, but she tended to panic at the sight of blood. Craig was the kind of rough and tumble boy who managed to shed a lot of it. Becca could empathise with nineteen-year-old Kaylee. She knew what it was like to feel the town's judgement on her capacity to mother her children.

Thank goodness the clinic was almost clear of patients this late in the afternoon. She averted her eyes from the bloody mess on the linoleum floor. It was near the automatic door at the front of the medical clinic and therefore an immediate hazard. The priority was the child but preventing an accident came close. This was the part of the job she was good at. Seeing what had to be done and expediting it. Fortunately, she had a great team.

In minutes Karen joined her, helping to secure the dressing. Rebecca was able to pry the three-year-old from his mother's arms, while Karen soothed her. Once in the treatment room, Craig settled down, his fears more due to his mother's emotional reaction than any pain from the cut.

The bleeding had slowed to a sluggish trickle. Quickly cleaning the wound and surrounding skin, Rebecca contemplated the evidence proving a little blood could go such a long way. Several smears marred the pale blue skirt of her uniform where his leg had brushed against it, but it was neither here nor there at this stage of the day. She'd be changing into jeans and a warm jacket to go home, once the clinic closed. Responding to Craig's chatter, she assured the boy he'd soon be mended as good as new.

As if on cue, a noise at the door told her help had arrived but she kept her eyes on what she was doing.

'Karen? Could you tell the doctor we'll need some stitches in treatment room two? Then you can finish with Mrs Cordery's dressing and we'll be done for the day. Barring another emergency.' There was a pause and she was about to repeat herself, when a voice spoke from the doorway. Most definitely not Karen.

'I think we can do better than stitches.'

Rebecca stiffened, then straightened, preparing to turn and face the intruder. There was something heart-stoppingly familiar in the low tones and for a few seconds she'd had a déjà vu moment. But this voice was deeper and rougher than the one she remembered.

'I beg your pardon?' It was him. Morgan Cavanaugh, two weeks early, and larger than life. If you could call six foot four of skin and bones in a loose grey sweater and faded jeans larger than life. His red hair was a beacon above the paleness of his skin, cut severely short, the slight curl hardly visible. Her eyes wanted to drink him in but she couldn't, wouldn't, give in to the urge, so she turned back to the boy. 'This is Doctor Cavanaugh, Craig. He's taking over here when Doctor Farrell goes to live on the Gold Coast, near his daughter.'

***

'Becca? Becca Bujold?' Morgan couldn't believe his eyes as he took in the petite figure in the neat blue uniform with navy trims. Where was the wild child with the long, dark mahogany hair and bewitching smile? Where were the sparkling brown eyes, the colour of his mother's best sherry? This uptight looking woman with the severely cropped hair looked like her, but not quite. The primly pursed mouth in a thin tanned face, eyes hidden behind narrow glasses, seemed like a woman with all life and joy sucked out of her.

'Rebecca Walters.'

Her voice came out flat and businesslike without the musical lilt he remembered. *Walters*. She must have married Dan and this was presumably what life with him had made of her. In those early years when the bitterness had eaten at him, he'd speculated on revenge, but it seemed fate had taken care of it for him. He wouldn't wish this result on his worst enemy, and whatever the past, Becca was too important to him to be considered an enemy.

She raised an eyebrow. 'You said something about doing better than stitches? Doctor Farrell usually puts a couple of stitches in a cut like this.' She was all business and he moved forward to look closely at the injury, thrusting aside his discomfort.

As he thought, it was a neat slicing cut, and not deep. 'I've been using a skin glue I find works well on this kind of wound. It's more expensive but will give a cleaner result. If you don't have any in stock I've a few samples in the car.'

'We do have some. We had a young locum the last time Doctor Farrell was on holiday, and she liked to use it for children. They use it all the time at the Mater Hospital apparently, but Doctor Farrell doesn't like it. Says he's too old to learn new tricks.'

Was there a slight twitch to her mouth at her last comment? He wasn't sure, but he wasn't given an opportunity to study her. She stepped briskly past him to open the cabinet, retrieving the Dermabond and selecting a fresh, disposable dressing tray. Watching her set up for the treatment, he had to admire her economical movements and neat manner of working. When she finished setting up, she stood aside to allow him room to manoeuvre, remaining within easy reach.

With a smile and quick word with the child, he pulled on the gloves laid out for him. After swabbing and drying the wound, he guided Becca's gloved hands into place to hold the sides of the cut together. He released them rather abruptly, oddly affected by the contact, and she looked up at him, brows wrinkling at his action. Morgan ignored the look, preparing the glue, but out of the corner of his eye he saw her shake her head slightly, as if clearing it. Almost immediately she focused on her job, watching carefully as he pinned the neatly joined skin with the glue.

Instructing her and the boy to hold still for a minute, he pulled off the gloves and disposed of them. 'When did you finish your RN training, Becca?' It was a courteous enough question so why did she flush scarlet under his glance? She'd always planned to become a nurse so it was hardly something new.

With a quick look at the child, who was studying the glued portion of his anatomy with great interest, she shook her head. 'I didn't do RN training. Just my Cert IV in Aged Care at the nursing home. Later on, I did business studies externally.'

'So why are you working as a clinic nurse?'

'I'm not. Karen's the clinic nurse. I help her out when it's busy.'

'You're a casual?'

'No. I work here full-time.' She seemed, if anything, more embarrassed. 'I'm the practice manager.'

He knew he was staring. Practice manager. Doc Farrell had mentioned how lucky he was with his staff. It hadn't occurred to him it would be Becca. He'd have to work closely with her every day. He'd go insane. Totally, mind bogglingly, insane.

*

Morgan stretched his legs out as he settled into the armchair in Doctor Farrell's office. It was good to relax, half the relief produced by the absence of Becca from the room. He was still stiff from the journey and standing hunched over the child while fixing the cut had made it worse. Or had it been the proximity to Becca tensing his neck and shoulders? He rubbed them, conscious of the intent look from the older man.

'Getting right into it already, Morgan.'

The rich rolling tone with the faintly Scottish accent was so familiar. Donald Farrell had delivered him, and most of the locals born in Maiden's Landing over the last forty years. Doc Barrell, he'd been called irreverently by the young people in sly reference to his shape, but with a fondness that recalled his patience and the store of sweets he kept in a jar on his desk. The jar was still there, but with stickers instead of the sugary treats. Becca's doing?

'It seemed logical when everyone was busy. I hope you didn't consider it encroaching.'

The other man laughed. 'I'm not likely to complain if it means I get to sit at my desk instead of chasing after newfangled glue to put the lad together.' He sobered. 'Seriously, I'm glad of it. I'm seventy next month and more than ready to retire.'

Morgan was aware of the doctor's upcoming knee surgery, but he respected his reticence. 'I'm sorry I couldn't get here sooner.'

'The important thing is you're here now. Still not looking fit, but I suppose it will come.' The shrewd eyes rested benevolently on Morgan's face, seeing more than Morgan wanted him to see.

'I'll be settling in over the next week or two, but I would like to come in each morning to familiarise myself with the practice.'

'By all means. Becca will be your main man to get you up to speed. She runs the computer system and the business side of things. I'd have been still using the old filing system but she nagged me into upgrading.' There was an element of satisfaction in the old boy's expression. He had always been fond of Becca, letting her do work experience at the practice during her last few years at school. It meant Morgan would be stuck with her.

As if he'd read Morgan's thoughts, Doc Farrell cleared his throat. 'All the staff are excellent. I hope you aren't planning any sweeping changes. Bert and Karen have been here for well-nigh twenty years and Becca's been running the place for eight years or so. Young Laureen on reception is new, but she fits in with the team. They all need the work. Not too many jobs available locally unless you're in agriculture and they mostly want backpackers for picking.'

'I didn't expect to see Becca still in town.'

There, he'd said it.

With a vague wave of a hand showing its age, the doctor smiled. 'With two kiddies to look after, she needed the support of the community. She'd have been a fool to move to the city where she knew no-one and everything is dearer. She's got her mother's old place still, out your way.'

'What about Dan?' Surely he'd be helping out financially. With two children. She must have had another child later.

'He's there with her. Works in Bialga so you won't see too much of him. Although you'll be neighbours, so to speak. Local gossip tells me you bought the property next to your parents. I think your mother was hoping to take you back under her wing and get you fattened up again.'

'I'm too old to go back to living with my parents. It's been close to fifteen years without counting boarding school. I like being on my own.'

A small crease marred the plump smoothness of the older man's forehead. 'I'm surprised you didn't bring a wife and family back with you.'

'I'm sure my mother would have been happy to see me settled before this. I liked my work and it wasn't conducive to relationships.' He didn't want to talk about himself, but his respect for the man he'd known all his life kept his resentment under control.

'I suppose not.' Doc Farrell steepled his fingers thoughtfully. 'Yes, I suppose it must be close to thirteen years since you were last home. I don't think I've seen you since the night of the tragedy.'

Something tightened in Morgan's chest. 'I did come back for the police interviews in Bialga, but only stayed overnight with my parents.'

'And we haven't seen you until today.'

'There was no reason to come back. My career was elsewhere.'

'Of course.' Those shrewd eyes were delving into his soul again. 'I think you'll find a lot of things have changed. You missed a lot while you were away. Maybe you'll find more than one reason to stay.'

Morgan wondered at the slow deliberation of the words. He couldn't help feeling the other man was trying to tell him something. A shiver prickled his spine. He'd had good reasons to leave and some of those reasons still existed. What on earth did the doctor think would encourage him to stay? He was committed to the practice and the contract with the local hospital was for three years. Enough time to get his own health back up to scratch. Unless he was concerned about Morgan's parents' health. But he already knew about his father's heart condition.

He had a feeling there was something else. An image of Becca flashed into his mind, the new Becca, so restrained and prim. He dismissed it. There was nothing here for him. Not anymore.

Chapter 2

It was a relief to climb on her bike and start peddling home, leaving Morgan to speak with Doctor Farrell. Morgan's parents waited at their home for her to pick up the children. If she could reach there and take the children before their son arrived all the better. The last thing she needed was another run in with Morgan Cavanaugh.

Twenty minutes later she leaned the bike against the bottom of the front steps of the Cavanaugh homestead. She was used to the five-kilometre ride, as were the children. Quickly mounting the stairs she went through to the kitchen, led by the sound of happy chatter. Grace Cavanaugh spotted her first, her attention drawn from the homework books spread over the old pine kitchen table.

'Rebecca? Home early for a change.'

The twins looked up with brows furrowed and she gave them a reassuring smile.

'I got away right on time. Morgan arrived and helped out with an emergency.'

Grace's taut expression showed her conflict. 'You've seen Morgan? What did he say?'

'He seemed surprised to see me. I thought he'd know.'

Grace flushed. 'I haven't mentioned you at all in my letters.'

Her husband stepped in, tipping the freshly peeled potatoes into the sink and frowned at his wife. 'You mean Morgan had no idea he'd be working with Becca at the clinic?'

'There never seemed the right time. I meant to tell him when he came here. It didn't occur to me he'd go straight to the clinic when he arrived in town.'

'Damn.' Becca slumped onto the end of the table, ignoring Grace's disapproving look at her language. 'What if he doesn't want me there? It's his practice after all.'

Ned Cavanaugh shook his head. 'Morgan wouldn't put you out of work without good reason, Becca. Everyone knows what a good job you do at the clinic.'

Pulling herself together, she gathered the children's books and slid them into their backpacks. 'Quickly, kids, we should get home before it gets dark.' She sent a meaning look at Grace as the children clattered their way down the back steps. 'We need to talk. About the twins coming here.'

'No hurry. I mean, there's no reason why Morgan would come here during clinic hours.'

Becca stared at the older woman. Did she want Morgan to find out? It had been twelve years of not acknowledging their true role, even if some people who remembered Morgan might have guessed.

Maybe she wanted the secrecy to end. Becca was long over it, but she'd given her word, so it was up to Grace to make the next move. Every now and then, the fear of turning into Grace woke Becca in a cold sweat. Yet how could she avoid it? The woman was the ultimate in respectable and Becca had spent too many years trying to gain her approval.

Evading Grace's worried gaze, she bade them goodnight, surprised when Ned guided her out to the front verandah. His face under the thick head of pure white hair was flushed, showing up the scarring where his fair skin had been treated for skin cancers. He'd given Morgan his colouring, only the long aristocratic nose coming from Grace's side of the family. The older woman's hair was still determinedly blonde, in a short streaky bob framing her narrow face with the faded brown eyes and thin lips.

Becca hesitated at the top step, staring across at the neighbouring property soon to house Morgan Cavanaugh. Too close for comfort.

'Seriously, Becca, don't let it get to you. Morgan is always fair.'

The silence hung in the air as Becca held her tongue, conscious of the children retrieving their bikes from the side of the house. Ned cleared his throat, his natural shyness showing in the mottled flush on his cheeks.

'I'm not sure exactly what went on between the two of you. But it was more than twelve years ago. You'd be a fool to hang onto a grudge for all that time.'

'No grudges on my part, Ned. You know I've always been grateful for the help you and Grace have been with the kids. You're the closest thing to grandparents they have after all.'

Sensing the irony in her statement, Ned didn't argue. 'We appreciate your sacrifices too, Becca. Don't ever doubt it.'

Shrugging, she mounted the bike as the two children waved and yelled out their farewells.

'Bye, Grandpa Ned, see you tomorrow.'

'See you tomorrow, billy lids. Bye, Becca.'

Reluctantly she smiled, seeing his worried face ease. 'See you tomorrow, Ned. And thanks for the reassurance.'

The winter sky still shone dusky blue as they made their way down the driveway and turned away from the town. The air seemed hazy, as if a car had recently stirred up the dust of the unpaved road. Instinctively, she searched out the Maiden place next door, seeing lights come on in the old homestead. Morgan was home.

Apparently, he didn't want to live with his parents. Grace had plenty to say on the subject, but it was interesting to note she didn't manage to overrule Morgan. There was no sign of a car, but he could easily have parked out of sight in one of the old sheds behind the house.

They must have missed him on his way home by minutes. With the two driveways so close, he could have seen her and the children easily, despite the encroaching winter twilight. Not sure if she were glad or sorry, she turned away from the road, down the rough, gravel-strewn track that served as a driveway.

Compared to the other properties across the road, the old fibro building with the battered, rust speckled roof was quite a comedown. She'd have liked to do more but keeping the mortgage under control took all her spare money. Grace had suggested she sell it and rent in town. Or further afield. It had been a tempting thought, especially once she had her qualifications.

A kelpie-cross barked enthusiastically from under the house and ran out to the length of the chain, ready to greet the children. Edward went to pat the panting dog, releasing her from the chain. Kirsty had been given to both the children but was his by proxy. Gabby yanked her backpack off the bike and tramped into the house with a pout that didn't bode well.

Grabbing her own bag from the carrier, Becca followed her daughter inside, puzzled about what brought on the moodiness in the usually equable girl. Her initial plan to deal with it straight up was halted when a crash came from the kitchen. Dumping the bag in the hall, she made her way to the back of the house.

The kitchen seemed empty at first, but a scuffling noise from the other side of the old red and white Laminex table alerted her to the source of the breakage.

'Hi, Dan. What's the problem?'

The man scrambled up, a good head taller than Becca and carrying extra weight on his midriff.

'I dropped the bickie barrel. I'm sorry, Bec.'

His hand swiped across his upper lip and automatically she handed him a tissue. It was pointless trying to remonstrate. He couldn't help his clumsiness. Tomorrow she'd buy a plastic container to replace the old china one dating from her childhood.

'Don't worry about it, Dan. I can cook some more tonight while you watch TV.'

Carefully steering him away from the shattered china and crushed biscuits, she sat him down at the table. 'What did you do at work today?'

'We sorted heaps of stuff. Gordon found a stack of old Bee Gee's records to put in the shop.'

He rambled on, listing the different items the charity run recycling depot had brought to light while Becca cleaned up the mess. At least Dan enjoyed working with his mates at the facility, which offered supervised employment opportunities to people with an intellectual disability.

Once the clean-up was done, it was time to serve dinner. Grateful she'd put the chicken and vegetables in the crockpot before heading to work, she ladled out the thick casserole onto the plates.

'Tea's ready. Edward, Gabby.'

The two eleven-year-olds jostled in the doorway and Becca had to laugh. Twins were supposed to be like two halves of a whole but these two were poles apart. Although shorter than his sister by a hand span, Edward was the eldest by several minutes and never let his taller, lankier sister forget it.

Apart from his natural older brother dominance, he was the quiet one of the two, studious and a little shy. Gabby lived up to her name, usually talkative and sociable, a leader in her small clique but still competing on a level field with her brother academically.

They were different in colouring too, Edward with the same dark mahogany hair and golden-brown eyes of his mother, while Gabby, with her brilliant blue eyes and bright red mop curling over her ears, bore no resemblance to anyone in her family.

Dan's blonde hair had a gingery tinge but there was no blood relationship, so it didn't count. With a twinge of anxiety, she looked over at Dan, wondering how he'd react to Morgan's return. He'd never mentioned his former friend in all the years since the accident. She wasn't sure if he remembered him.

He did remember some things. He talked about the horse at the Maiden place and going blackberrying on the ridge behind the Cavanaugh homestead. She had to drag him out of the creek where the Durand's property joined up with the national park a couple of times a month, mostly during the summer. Usually muddy and fully clothed and disappointed about not catching any yabbies.

He finished the chicken and she handed him a spoon to eat the gravy. Only a few more weeks and the responsibility would end. The department had promised when they finished building the new supported accommodation at Bialga that there'd be a place for Dan. It was only a few blocks from the recycling depot and would save him the half hour bus trip each way. All his friends lived in the neighbouring town and there were more opportunities to socialise in the larger centre.

The opening to speak to Gabby came at the sink once Dan had vanished into his room to watch television. Edward took himself to the bedroom he shared with his sister to snatch some quiet time with his model making. They took it in turns to do the drying and Becca was grateful for the privacy the task gave her with each of the children. She was lucky to have her work at the clinic, but it meant less time in the evenings at home.

'What's it about, Gabby?'

'What's what about?'

So, it was going to be a battle. 'Something's bothering you. You've been sour on and off all evening.'

'There's nothing you can do about it.'

Becca seriously wondered if the china would survive as the plates rattled onto the shelf. Whatever had her daughter so worked up must be more serious than usual.

With a faint sigh she placed the heavy stoneware bowl on the rack. 'How about you tell me, and we'll see if we can find a solution.'

'You can't. It's for the working bee on next Saturday. They want all the fathers to go. They plan to redo all the gardens. You couldn't move one of those old sleepers they've got around the edges.'

Which was a massive understatement all things considered. Becca remembered the note coming home from the school. She planned to go, even if she made sandwiches and brewed tea and coffee for the workers. But it was the father thing bugging Gabby. Over the past year, more and more she'd displayed resentment when school functions required the presence of a father. Not that they were the only single parent family in town. Becca knew of several, including a single dad she remembered from school. People had tried to match them up.

Studying her daughter's face, with the distinctive blue eyes above the overly long nose, Becca had a momentary qualm. But she had no options. Her path had been laid out for her nearly twelve years ago when she'd been forced into a choice that was no choice at all. Morgan's return had only made it more imperative.

Everything had changed the night of the accident. They'd all been supposed to go to a party but it had turned into a blazing row instead, the moment Dan had left with his friends. She'd tried to explain, but she couldn't tell him everything. Not knowing Dan would be back and would take it out on her in his usual way. It hadn't mattered. Morgan preferred to believe Dan. They'd faced each other like bitter enemies for minutes that seemed like hours, until Morgan turned away dismissively, thrusting her away when she'd clung. She'd washed his touch from her skin fiercely, as if she could wash away the accusations. Washing away the tears, because she wouldn't, couldn't let Morgan know how his words had hurt.

Later, when he cooled down, she thought he'd see things differently. But first came the accident and there hadn't been a later. He'd avoided her at Brittany's funeral. The anger and disillusionment on his face had almost broken her heart. But it had taken his cold disdain afterwards to shatter it completely. At least her heart had stopped aching then. All that was left of it, an empty void and a tightness that sometimes woke her up breathless at night.

He'd gone back to Brisbane instead of staying for Christmas like usual. When she'd visited the homestead, Grace told her they planned on staying at the Gold Coast for the holidays. He'd changed his mobile number and her emails vanished into the ether.

The death of her mother shortly before the birth of the twins hadn't stirred any feelings. Except perhaps a small amount of relief there would be no more pain for Emmy Bujold. She had known far too much suffering in her relatively short life. She'd been thirty-five, only six years older than Becca's age now. Three years older than Morgan.

Eventually she'd rung Grace from the hospital in Brisbane after the twin's premature birth. They'd struck the deal outside the paediatric intensive care unit after Grace had inspected the children. She'd acknowledged Morgan's paternity without argument. Expecting a denial, Becca had agreed to her conditions without real thought for the future, grateful only that Gabby and Edward would be safe and cared for. She'd already accepted Morgan wasn't going to be a part of their lives for the foreseeable future, so Grace's conditions hadn't seemed so difficult.

She'd given him her heart when she'd been just sixteen, perhaps long before, adoring him from the fringes of the neighbourhood clique. In return he treated her gently, not yelling at her like the other kids did when she followed them on their private excursions. He'd taught her to ride and let her drive the old ute around the property occasionally. She'd been too short at first so he'd had to do the pedals with her sitting on his lap doing the steering. As time passed, they'd spent hours together at his home, watching movies and talking books. Outside, he'd more or less ignored her in favour of his friends and his occasional short-lived girlfriends, until he went to boarding school, presumably finding distraction with the city girls.

When he came home for the holidays not long after she'd turned sixteen, he suddenly seemed to notice her as a girl. Teasing her, paying her small attentions and compliments. Still busy with his studies, he only came home occasionally, but he kept in touch by email and text. They talked about the future, compared ambitions and found them compatible, Morgan planning to be a doctor and Becca would be training as a registered nurse. Together they dreamed of travelling the world, using their skills in third world countries. Implicit in all was the suggestion they'd be man and wife.

It hadn't been easy, nourishing a relationship on emails and phone calls and irregular visits. No wonder when they came together after months apart, they'd been unable to control the passion that flared between them. A weekend of loving exploration ending too quickly with his return to Brisbane. There'd been one more weekend they'd spent together and then she'd not seen him again until the fatal night when her heart had taken such a beating.

Only the birth of her children had mended it. In part, anyway. Part of it had gone forever, along with her youthful confidence and what little had remained of her trust in men. Morgan had been the one man she'd trusted. The one man she'd believed she could be herself with. To show her affectionate side. Which had worked against her in the end. He'd thought she was like that with other men. With Dan.

Becca shuddered, remembering the day Dan had caught her throwing up and asked if she was pregnant. She'd denied it but he'd realised she'd slept with Morgan. He'd been livid, his jealousy of Morgan fuelled to violence by his substance abuse, not being careful to keep his blows to places hidden by her clothes. She'd known at that moment she'd have to do something. Keeping her ailing mother free of stress wasn't worth the risk when she had her baby to consider. Without Dan's mother helping care for her mum, Becca could see her chances of finishing school dwindling to nothing but the cost was too high.

Then the accident happened and it all changed. Everything changed.

Now, confronted by her eleven-year-old daughter, the confidence she'd struggled so hard to rebuild wavered. She wondered whether the quieter Edward had the same fears and insecurities. Whether he felt short-changed by their situation. It wasn't easy for any of them, living with Dan's foibles. The house was tiny, with three smallish bedrooms, kitchen, bathroom and long narrow lounge room that was actually a closed in verandah.

The logical answer was for Becca to find a stepfather for the children. Someone who wouldn't mind being an instant father. Grace had been trying to encourage her into a relationship for years. Probably in anticipation of Morgan's eventual return. No doubt she still harboured fears Becca could lure the Cavanaugh pride and joy back into her web of destruction. They had no idea of how impossible that would ever be. In the wisdom of hindsight, her own hopes of long ago were totally naïve. Morgan would never forgive her for her supposed betrayal.

For herself, the thought of letting a man into her life made her cringe. Intellectually she knew men were not all tarred with the same brush, but after her experience with her stepfather and Dan pre-accident, it would take a special man to make her reconsider her single status. She was doing fine by herself. It wasn't always easy, but it was better than the alternative. She wasn't going to risk her children going through the same things she'd had to put up with growing up.

In the meantime, she could see no immediate solution. 'I'll be taking sandwiches and biscuits in. It's the best I can do, Gabby. Grandpa Ned isn't strong enough to lift sleepers either.'

The sulky moue on the girl's lips didn't reassure, but the washing up didn't actually involve any breakages so she could be grateful for small mercies.

Tucking the pair of them into bed later, she remembered the conversation. Remembered wondering about Edward. He hadn't said anything but he wasn't a chatty boy at the best of times. The model ship lay on the desk with several pieces scattered around beside the half-finished hull. An uncapped bottle of glue sat rather drunkenly on a book. Usually he tidied up straight away but Becca suspected the challenge of building the sailing ship left him frustrated.

She rummaged around to find the lid and put it back on the glue bottle, straightening the desk automatically. Why tonight, of all nights? Gabby's complaint should have been enough to deal with, yet in his own way, her son also cried out for a father. She tried to help him with his models, but he resisted. Without asking, Becca knew the models were a statement of masculinity in his female dominated world. He needed a man to spend time with him. To help him with the models, and to be a role model. Ned Cavanaugh did his best but his age and health impacted on what he could do with a small active boy.

Wryly she acknowledged the truth. The consciousness of what the children needed wasn't new. But Morgan's presence in town made the awareness acute. If things had been different, he would have been the father of her children in reality, not just biologically. The man they needed in their life. The man she had hoped for, truth be told. There had been no-one else for her in all those years, in spite of the matchmaking attempts of friends and neighbours. With the eyes of the town on her, she couldn't afford to slip up again. The children would be the ones to suffer from gossip. Morgan wasn't the answer. He hadn't loved her. At least not enough to believe in her. She'd given him her trust, hard won. He'd failed to return it.

Brushing a strand of hair from Edward's forehead she smiled down at him, meeting sleepy eyes that matched her own. 'Love you, Mum.'

'Love you too, baby.' He didn't protest as usual at the endearment, his lips curving in a faint smile as he let sleep overtake him.

Gabby lay sprawled across her bed, already asleep, her long legs and arms splayed like a pale spider. Covering her up took some energy, thrusting the wayward limbs back under the covers. The winter morning temperatures could be low in the high country.

In her own room, she stripped and pulled on the old t-shirt she used as a night dress. Thin almost to the point of indecency, it covered down to her knees. Years ago, when Grace cleaned out Morgan's old clothes and passed them over, the older woman probably thought only of Dan. She would be disturbed if she knew Becca wore them to bed.

And rightly so. What kind of sick puppy clings to her ex-boyfriend's old t-shirts and wears them to bed as part of her fantasy life?

Considering the state of her love life, non-existent to negative in quantity, it said far too much about the state of her shrivelled heart.

Sure, she loved her kids, she was fond of Ned Cavanaugh and tolerated his wife. Respected her even. With Dan, there would always be an ambivalence around what he'd tried to do and the price he'd paid.

Slipping between the cool sheets, Becca sighed with relief as she coiled herself into a comfortable position on the lumpy mattress. This was one of those times she could be grateful for her small size and light weight. Replacing the mattress and maybe the bedframe had been on her to-do list forever. It seemed likely to remain there.

Especially if Morgan decided he didn't want to work with her at the clinic. It could easily happen, if the look of horror on his face when she'd stated her job position were any indication. Hours later her chest tightened painfully at the thought of his repugnance at working with his former teen girlfriend. But she wouldn't cry. She never cried. Not once in twelve years had she let a tear escape from sometimes burning eyes.

They thought her cold, the people in town, but she worked hard all these years to earn their respect. No-one could say she didn't pull her weight, working long hours at the clinic when necessary, volunteering at the school, attending church without fail every Sunday, the kids scrubbed to within an inch of their lives. Her mother had been pitied but not respected.

Respect was worth far more than pity and there's no way on earth she'd let anyone pity her.

***

Cursing the fuse box, Morgan replaced the wire for the kitchen power points. First thing tomorrow he'd have to get an electrician out. It was a beautiful old timber homestead, with the wide verandah and elegant steps of a former era, but it hadn't had an update in decades. Probably since long before he was born. He'd played with the Maiden kids as a child but they'd all left town once they finished school and their parents had followed a few years later, selling out to an investment company. They'd leased the land out to local farmers but let the building rot.

It had been an impulse to buy the property, spotting it on the real estate agent's website when he'd been looking for a rental. Renovating it would give him something to do with his time when he was off duty. He'd have to do some socialising in his role as local doctor and hospital superintendent, but he had no intention of picking up the social links from his school years. Long before the breakup with Becca, he'd lost touch with his classmates, doing most of his socialising in Brisbane with his fellow medical students.

Shutting the metal box, he grabbed the torch and headed across the paddock to the spot on the fence where he'd crossed many a time on his way to hang with the Maiden boys. His mother had promised him a meal and with the stove not working and the fridge still warm after the power outage, it was his best option.

He'd barely arrived at the back door when his mother appeared, tears glinting in her eyes, caught in the outside light over the back stairs.

'Morgan.'

Her arms wrapped around him in an unusual display of affection. She'd lost weight in the long months since they'd last seen each other. She gripped his upper arms and drew him into the kitchen. 'Let me look at you.'

Her sharp eyes scanned his face while her fingers poked and prodded at his ribs. 'You look dreadful.'

'Thanks, Mum.'

She frowned at his wry tone and pursed her lips. Biting her tongue, no doubt. 'You know we're concerned. Doctor Farrell told us how dangerous your pneumonia could have been if you hadn't been treated.'

'I'm almost recovered. It wasn't bad. It was more about where I was at the time. I was at a clinic in a fairly isolated part of the country.' He shook off her hold and reached a hand to his father, who hovered in the background. 'Dad?'

'It's good to see you, son.'

They'd never been a demonstrative family, but his father's grip told him more than the conventional words what it meant to him to have his son home. Guilt niggled at Morgan. Knowing of his father's health issues, this homecoming was long overdue.

There was no time for more as Grace bustled them into the dining room, ablaze with the best silver and crockery. This was a welcome home with a vengeance. All his favourite foods, roast lamb and vegetables and apple crumble and custard for dessert.

'You're trying to fatten me up.'

Grace nodded. 'I do think you'd be better to stay with us until the Maiden place is fixed up. You know I love to cook.'

'I'm happy there. It's not like I've been living in luxury these last years.'

He was grateful for the change of subject as his father asked him about the places he'd been working and the living conditions. By the time they were drinking coffee in the lounge, Grace seemed resigned to him being a neighbour, insisting he come home and eat the evening meal. 'At least until you get properly settled.'

The anxious expression on his father's face made him agree and he was rewarded by his look of quiet satisfaction.

He'd been back at his new home for an hour, after fighting with the gas hot water system for his shower, when it occurred to him that among all the people they'd reminisced about, Becca's name had never been mentioned. Which seemed odd, considering they had to be aware she'd be working with him at the clinic. He went to sleep on the thought and entered into strange dreams that had haunted him for over a decade. Dreams where Becca smiled at him with the glow which had been noticeably absent on their first meeting after all those years.

Chapter 3

The waiting room overflowed with pensioners who'd come in late for their annual flu jabs, so it wasn't a good time for a car accident to require the presence of a surgeon at the hospital. Not that any time was good for an accident.

In a small town, the tragedies seemed to hit home, creating ripples impacting the entire community. Becca sighed heavily as she prepared the treatment room for the onslaught. While the injections themselves only took a few moments, each and every one of the elderly patients would be ready for a chat.

Already the buzz circulating around town had the new doctor in its sights. The speculation about his marital status had been the first one to hit her as she assisted Laureen behind the desk only two days after he arrived in town. Rumours about a fatal disease he'd picked up in the Amazon.

'No, Doctor Cavanaugh has recently come back from Central Africa.'

'Yes, he would be the new consultant surgeon at the hospital replacing Doctor Farrell.'

'No, they wouldn't let him back into the country if he had anything contagious.'

And over and over again, as if they wanted to remind her, though most people didn't know for sure about their relationship. 'No, I don't know if Doctor Cavanaugh is married.'

'Yes, it's true he bought the Maiden place.'

'It is a large family home. But I've no idea of his plans.'

Beryl Harmsworth was there of course, her smug smile and curious gaze watching everything. It was a pity she hadn't married and had children and grandchildren of her own to keep her occupied. She'd reminded Becca of Miss Gulch on her bicycle from *The Wizard of Oz* when she was growing up. It was hard to overcome her early prejudice, especially as Becca had proven the old lady's predictions of coming to a bad end with her teenage pregnancy and no father in sight. The old woman had speculated quite loudly at the time. Only her fear of Grace Cavanaugh's displeasure had kept her from actively naming Morgan as a potential culprit. Because Morgan had only been home during holidays in those last few years before the twins were born, the old gossip hadn't been sure and Becca had kept out of her way as far as possible in those early years. Much as Becca hated the thought, she'd benefited from the big scandal around Brittany Smith's death which allowed her to stay under the radar during her pregnancy.

By the time the local gossips noticed Becca had somehow acquired two children Morgan was long gone and he hadn't come back. Until now.

This morning, three days after his arrival, there would be more speculation, more curious questions. If someone asked her one more time if Morgan had a wife, or intended to get married, she'd probably scream. Already the muscles at the back of her neck and shoulders were tense, her stomach churning. He'd been in several times to see Doctor Farrell but she'd been out and about, at the pharmacy and up at the hospital mostly. One time she'd been out at old Bob McIntyre's place, checking his blood sugar readings.

Knowing tomorrow Morgan would be in the office most of the day, learning the computer system and database, increased her tension exponentially. Familiarising himself with case files and the claims system would require her to spend a good percentage of her time with him, one on one. She could only hope his time spent on the fringes of civilisation hadn't made him averse to adopting the latest technology.

Convincing Doctor Farrell to update the systems had been the work of years of persuasion on her part. He'd finally given in five years ago, on the grounds it would make the practice more appealing for a new doctor. The decision to retire had been made long before, but luring city doctors out from larger centres took more than selling them on fresh air and a country lifestyle. At least Morgan would reap the benefit of the upgrade.

Hopefully, it wouldn't be the last achievement before Becca was out on her ear.

She was about to send the first of the flu jab appointments through to the treatment room when a prickle of unease alerted her to an arrival through the back entrance of the clinic. She didn't need to look to know it was Morgan. It had been like this when she was an infatuated teenager, always sensitive to his presence. His warm breath was on her left ear, the heat of his body close behind her. It was fortunate she'd had plenty of practice not flinching.

'Do you need some help? I left Doctor Farrell at the hospital.'

'Is everyone okay?'

Her chest tightened waiting for the response. After all these years, she was automatically thrown back in time to the night Brittany Smith had died.

'One girl was airlifted to Sydney with spinal injuries, but the rest were only minor cuts and bruises.'

She opened her mouth to ask who when a stir among the waiting patients distracted her.

Morgan made a choking noise. 'Who the hell is that?'

'Thackery Harmsworth.'

'Seriously?'

Thackery was meandering through the waiting room, seemingly unaware of the stares of the rest of the occupants. He wore a close-fitting fake fur trimmed woman's coat and denim flares that dated to the seventies. The coat hung open showing a patchwork vest in vibrant silks. Dark brown dreadlocks hung in frizzy coils to his shoulders and flicked with each twist as he worked his way past the seated patients. 'He gets most of his clothes at the op-shop.'

'Not a local?'

'He is, kind of. You wouldn't remember him. He wandered into town about ten years ago to start high school. He lives with his sister on the organic farm at the end of our road. Against the national park.'

'Old Ray Harmsworth's place? He's related to that family?'

'Ray's grandkids.'

By this time, the whole of the room was focused on the young man who approached Beryl Harmsworth with a wry smile on his darkly tanned face. 'Hello, Aunty Beryl.'

Beryl Harmsworth had lost the smug expression, her pale eyes chilly with disdain and her mouth compressed.

Thackery laughed and with a smile and wink for Becca, headed back to the reception desk, his light green eyes vivid against tanned skin as he leaned on the counter, his fatal smile focused on Laureen. 'I have an appointment.'

Becca watched Beryl make her way out of the surgery, chin high and her eyes focused on safety. Morgan gave a soft snort of laughter and she turned in surprise, meeting his bright blue gaze.

He shrugged. 'It's nice to see "Aunty Beryl" lost for words for a change. How exactly are they connected? I know Ray was her brother.'

'He's her great-nephew. Ray's eldest son married a Tanya Thompson from Bialga and moved away.'

'He's a character. I've never seen anyone face off to her like that.'

'He's a nice person too. He spends a lot of time with Dan and the children.'

'And you?'

'He's a good friend. The kind you can rely on.'

Morgan stiffened and she wondered if he'd taken it as a criticism. She hadn't meant it to be. Thackery was the best friend she had. He'd ignored her off-putting manner when the twins were small and insinuated himself into their lives with a casual ease that had disarmed her. He understood her sense of alienation from the community yet he didn't appear to let it bother him, even as a teenager. She envied him that careless disregard for public opinion.

With a glance at his watch, Morgan seemed to collect himself, the last of his smile fading and a chill to rival Beryl's cooling his gaze. 'I'll use Doctor Farrell's office and you can send anyone through who doesn't want to wait.'

Becca watched him go, faintly bemused by the small moment of connection. Somewhere inside, the Morgan she knew from the past was struggling to get out. Or maybe it was only with her he maintained a cold shell.

Doctor Farrell arrived back as Becca was seeing the last of the patients out the door. She flicked the switch to disarm the automatic slider and flipped the sign to closed. Morgan had gone once he dealt with all the urgent cases, leaving the vaccinations and a couple of wound treatments for Karen to take care of.

The older man flopped down on the armchair in his office with a groan, rubbing his right knee.

'Only a couple of days to go.'

'I thought it was two weeks?' Becca perched on the edge of his desk.

He sighed. 'Morgan is going to take over full-time on Monday. My surgeon wants me down there early for some tests.'

'Morgan's all right with starting early?'

'He suggested it. I was going to put the tests off, but Morgan reckons he can take over no problem.'

'Is he healthy enough?' He'd looked tired by the time he finished up with the patients.

The doctor observed her under lowered lids. 'He'll be able to cope. There'll be no elective surgery for a few weeks. I'd already organised for the visiting resident in Bialga to fill in for the time I was expecting to be away for my knee surgery. I left it at that. Morgan did a good job up at the hospital. I only had to deal with the paperwork.'

'Who was the spinal injury?'

'Tory Dibble. Jeanette's girl.'

Becca knew Jeanette, who was in Morgan's grade at school, but her daughter was older than the twins, so she didn't know her except by sight. 'How bad?'

'She'll have a long road. It could have been worse.' He shot a weary smile at her. 'No brain injury.'

Becca drooped in relief. She understood how hard it was. Not as hard as the Smith's though, who had lost Brittany in the same accident as Dan's injury. 'Tony's back in town. For Ashleigh's wedding.' Another of their classmates. She wondered if Morgan was going to the ceremony.

The doctor raised his brows. 'Tony? Poor kid. The accident really cut him up. I never expected him to come back, although his family's here. How do you know? Or do I need ask?'

'Beryl must have had her spies out.'

'That woman needs to pull her head in. Between her and Lynne at the post office, they have a monopoly on the gossip in this town.'

Becca could feel herself shrivelling.

'Don't let her get to you, girl. She's got nothing to use against you.'

'No. Not now.' Although with Morgan back in town, it might stimulate her memories of the past and she wasn't afraid to make sly innuendos. The most important thing was to keep Morgan away from the twins. Having them at Morgan's parents' place after school was asking for trouble. But they were too young to be latchkey kids and her only other friend who might be able to take them lived too far out of town.

Hopefully, once Morgan began work full-time at the surgery, there would be minimal chance of him coming across the children. Gabby especially would be curious. She was too clever not to add all the clues together. It had probably been a mistake letting the twins spend so much time at the Cavanaugh's place. They could easily have figured things out already. Which might explain the constant angst from Gabby.

***

Morgan walked slowly across the paddock, heading for his parents' place. He hadn't seen as much of them as he'd intended. The old homestead was sound but organising the plumbing and electrical work was a priority if the place wasn't to burn to the ground. In his spare time, between getting to know his new job, he'd had to do numerous minor repairs. It was hard to admit, but the physical work was tiring. He simply didn't have the stamina for sustained effort. Yet. He had to be patient. A lesson in the learning.

A couple of kids on bikes were pedalling up the driveway and he watched curiously. His father had mentioned something about looking after a neighbour's children after school while their mother was at work, but this was the first he'd seen of them. It surprised him. Grace wasn't a motherly type, at least not with other people's children.

A tall girl around twelve or thirteen, red hair showing under her pink bike helmet, led the way. She was closely followed by a younger boy with dark hair. They were already at the house by the time he threw a leg over the strip of rubber tubing that protected him from the barbed wire at the top of the fence which separated his new property from his old home. A gate was on the list of renovations, but not as urgent as making the house safe to live in.

He strolled past the two bikes leaning against the side of the house, making for the kitchen door in the footsteps of the younger visitors. He'd always liked children. There'd been far too many needing treatment during his sojourn in the rural areas of Rwanda and the other countries he'd worked in over the last few years. He'd been lucky to get an internship with a specialist in tropical medicine which meant he'd been able to head overseas after only a year doing his residency. It had made all the difference, considering his mental state in those few years after leaving Maiden's Landing.

The gabble of young voices told him the children were in the kitchen and he pushed the door open. He met his mother's startled gaze and hesitated, but she recovered quickly and smiled. 'Morgan, do come in.'

Silence greeted him from the young fry, two pairs of wide eyes, one blue and one pair a disturbingly familiar brown. Becca's eyes.

His mother paused in pulling biscuits out of the oven. 'This is Gabby and this young man is Edward.'

'Walters.' Morgan supplied the surname automatically. Becca's children. He'd thought he would be the father of her children. Eventually. They'd planned on a family, once both of them had finished their studies and had done their bit for the world. There'd always been the possibility of coming back home and taking over the clinic from Doctor Farrell. Now he was doing it alone. Except Becca was there too. Out of reach. Mother of these children and wife to another man.

He focused on his mother. 'I thought I might join you for afternoon tea.'

'We have to do some homework first,' a young voice piped up.

The girl. Gabby. He studied her lanky frame and bright head of hair. There was a familiarity nudging his memory, but he couldn't place it. She could have been his, going on the colouring, if he hadn't known better. He couldn't see a resemblance to either Dan or Becca in the long narrow face.

'I can wait. What are you doing?'

'Maths.' It came out with a roll of those expressive eyes. He glanced up as his father came into the room meeting a pair of faded blue eyes. Something jolted in his gut as he compared the two. No, the shape was different and the girl's mouth was fuller. Her nose was long. Like his? Something almost like disappointment sent bile to the back of his throat. He was an idiot. Still hankering for the past. All the same, something drew him to find out more.

He sat down beside the girl. 'Do you like maths?'

'It's okay.' She showed him the worksheet she'd pulled out of her backpack along with a brightly coloured pink pencil case. The boy, Edward, was doing the same, his pencil case a more modest dark green tartan. Morgan felt the curious gaze of both children.

Gabby had a frown pulling together the bright ginger brows as she studied him. A stranger in their midst. 'You know my mother, don't you?'

'Yes.' He didn't know what to say under her speculative gaze. He could hardly say he might have been her father. She was part of a family unit. He couldn't be a part of wrecking a family out of his own bitterness, if what he half suspected were true. Nausea churned in his gut.

If it were true it meant he'd made a terrible mistake. Yet there was the younger boy to prove she'd moved on with Dan. Gabby's existence didn't mean he'd been wrong about something happening between her and Dan back then. It hadn't been hard to believe Dan's hints. There'd always been an edginess in Becca's reactions to her step-cousin that he'd wondered about. All the same, her mistake, if it was one, could be forgiven in the circumstances. Although forgiving himself might come harder.

It came back to her age. She'd been sixteen and he'd dumped her without giving her a chance to explain. At nineteen he'd been the older one. The 'grown-up'. Maybe she hadn't had a choice once he'd abandoned her. The familiar blackness nudged at the back of his mind. *Not this time.* He steadied his breathing.

Gabby opened her mouth as if to ask another question and stopped suddenly, her eyes shifting away, dropping to her schoolwork.

His mother hurried into the breach looking oddly anxious, her fingers twisting the tea towel in her hands. 'This is my son, Morgan. You can call him Doctor Cavanaugh.'

'Morgan will be fine. Doctor Cavanaugh is such a mouthful.'

After her initial caution, Gabby seemed happy to chatter as she worked on her sums. Edward stayed quiet, his brows drawn together in concentration. At the end of the half hour, taking an Anzac biscuit from the plate his mother offered, Morgan was surprised how much he'd enjoyed the time with the children.

His parents surprised him too, with their obvious fondness for Becca's children. His mother had barely tolerated 'that Bujold girl'. His father wasn't so surprising. He'd always been kind to the small Becca when she'd hung around on the fringes of Morgan's group of friends. He'd had a few classmates as friends but they'd fallen away once he went to boarding school. The ones that had stuck were Dan and his mate Ben Smith and Ben's older brother Shane. The Smith boys lived on the other side of town but they'd all known each other forever because of Dan and Becca living across the road and the Smiths being related to the Maiden kids.

It had all changed with the accident. Ben and Shane had gone to Gatton to study agriculture whereas Morgan was in Brisbane because of his interest in tropical medicine at the faculty there. Dan and Becca had been lost to him because of their betrayal.

He pushed away the memories to focus on Gabby, who was asking him questions about Africa. The boy had vanished somewhere with

Ned, heading out the back door. Morgan could sense his mother hovering.

'If you've got something to do, I'm quite okay, Mum.'

'If you're sure. I should bring in the washing.'

He wasn't used to seeing his mother nervous. It made him wonder again as he watched the animated little face explaining about her plans for high school next year. He vaguely remembered her birthday would have been somewhere about now. His parents had come down to Brisbane once his uni exams were finished and they'd travelled to the Sunshine Coast for the holidays. He'd desperately needed the break after the stress of the previous six months.

His parents hadn't mentioned Becca, but he'd bumped into Jeanette and her mother on the beach with her toddler and they'd been updating him with the local news. Twelve years ago. His throat hitched at the thought of what that toddler would be going through now. Jeanette was a strong woman. She'd had to be. But seeing her teenager so badly injured must be heartbreaking.

He couldn't imagine how he'd cope. Gabby had fallen silent after his mother left the room and he wondered if she was nervous, left alone with a stranger. A family friend by proxy. Her mouth pursed in concentration; she was doodling on a scrap of paper.

'Do you want to be left alone, Gabby?'

'No.' The sharp answer surprised him, along with the way the pencil scratched across the paper onto the tablecloth.

She was looking at him again with that narrowed gaze. 'Did you know my mother at school?'

'I was older than her. We weren't in the same class.'

'Where you in Dan's class then?'

'I'm older than Dan and your mother.' It seemed disrespectful for her to call her father by his first name, but it wasn't his business.

'But you did know her then.'

'Yes.'

She was fiddling with her pencil again, flipping it over and over between the fingers of her left hand. 'Did you know my dad?'

There was something in the way she avoided his eyes that screamed caution. 'I've known Dan pretty much my whole life. I remember him as a little kid before he and his mother came to live with your mum.'

'He's not related to us, you know. His dad died before he was born. Then his mum married Mummy's uncle. He died too. Like...'

She stopped again, a pink flush washing over her pale skin. Like his. No freckles, only a chalky paleness he knew burnt and peeled in the hot Australian sun. He'd had problems with it in Africa, long before the skin condition took hold which had been one of the reasons for him coming home.

Maybe that was why she didn't call him Dad. Because she knew he wasn't.

'What did your mum tell you about your birth dad?'

'Nothing, really. She said I looked like him. Just exactly like him.' Her pale lashes fluttered as she peeked up at him from under them. 'I always wanted to meet him.'

Morgan bit his tongue. He'd learned a few interesting curses while working overseas. Not something he needed to introduce to this child. *His child?* His heart pounded like a drum, hard and fast. He gulped down the coil of barbed wire in his throat.

'You need to talk to your mother about it.'

She smiled, and it was her mother's smile in his own face. How did Becca think she could get away with it? Or had she counted on him never coming home? A sudden surge of anger closed his throat.

Gabby continued with a hushed tone. 'It's supposed to be a secret, I think. Except for

Grandpa Ned and your mum.' There was an almost wistful gleam in her eyes. 'It could be our secret.'

A secret. He wanted to grab her and hold her tight, this child he'd never expected. Twelve years stood between any hope she'd accept that kind of affection from her absent father. Brought up with secrets that must have hurt.

Had his parents ever acknowledged their grandchild?

They were obviously close, being treated as grandchildren, without the formalities. Certainly the affection was there for Ned. Grace held herself back, and the children must have read her distance and treated her with a similar reticence.

He forced a smile, hiding the seething volcano of emotion bubbling underneath. 'I guess we both need to talk to your mum.'

'Are you angry?'

Her eyes were wide and unblinking, perhaps a little afraid of what she'd unleashed.

'No, pumpkin. I'm surprised I wasn't let in on the secret.'

'Grace said...' The girl stumbled to a halt, biting her bottom lip.

'Yes?'

'I wasn't supposed to hear.'

'If you think you shouldn't repeat it, it's all right. I can ask my mum.'

'It was something about you being sick back then. That you should be allowed to get better. Are you very sick?'

Morgan debated how open to be to a child of her age, but she was too bright for evasions. He could give her a half-truth without compromising the past. 'I was sick and I'm still not fully healed. Like a bad flu. Overall, I'm good. I need to take it easy and not do too much for a while.'

Her face fell.

'I'm okay, Gabby.'

She screwed up her face. 'It was just I had a favour to ask.'

Chapter 4

Morgan was in a strange mood. The grey suit with the narrow dark pinstripe screamed professional but also distant. It camouflaged the lean body that had shocked her the first day with its angularity and prominent bones.

Becca was constantly aware of the way he stared at her when he thought she wasn't looking. She wondered if Morgan's distraction was for the same reason she'd been studying him covertly. She'd been a fool to think she could keep her secrets once Morgan returned. Even Grace had been doubtful, speculating on what might happen. They still hadn't come to an agreement about childcare and now it was too late. Grace seemed to think it better to let things go on as they were until Morgan asked. She still hadn't released Becca from the agreement though she had to know Morgan wouldn't let things lie. Not when he knew the truth, if Gabby's report of their conversation was correct.

It was hard to concentrate but they'd still managed to get a lot done. He was a quick study on the computer system, and he'd brought his own laptop along to integrate it into the network. All he needed was some practice to learn the protocols and he could work on it in his own time. That was the least of her worries.

It was nearly lunchtime and he'd be gone, according to the arrangements he'd made with Doc Farrell. She shifted, ready to make her excuses and leave.

Morgan raised his eyes from the laptop screen. 'I was wondering if you would have lunch with me. There are a few things I'd like to talk to you about.'

A chill kept her feet glued to the floor. 'Lunch?'

He glanced at his watch. 'It is lunchtime, isn't it?'

'Yes. But I don't see...'

His pale eyes narrowed. 'I'm not asking for a date. There are things I want to talk to you about the practice and I thought it would save time if we did it over a quick bite.'

Well, didn't she feel stupid. 'Of course. Where were you thinking?'

'The Regal? If it's still there.'

'Yes. It's changed a bit since your day, but the food is still good.'

Morgan frowned as he followed her out onto the street. 'Does Allison Goulas still own it?'

Becca paused to do up her long navy coat and she could see he was conscious of passers by having a good look at him.

'Yes. I think she'll die in the place. It's her precious. She did it up a few years ago. Once the town started to get a bit touristy. You'll hardly recognise it.'

He was silent as they turned the corner and headed along the main street. The ancient leopard trees with their distinctive bark still cast a wide shade from the centre strip. They'd been pruned to keep the branches from drooping low enough to affect traffic, but not as badly as the ones in the side streets along the footpaths that were under the power lines. 'I've often thought the original town planners must have had grandiose visions for Maiden's Landing with these wide streets and the median strips.'

Morgan stopped to stare at the trees, shoving his hands into his pockets. All the trees along the blocks that comprised the main shopping centre had lights strung over them, unlit during the day. 'It's funny. I haven't been home during the winter since before I graduated.'

'And here you are.'

He raised his brows. 'Do I note a sarcastic tone?'

With a shrug, Becca moved away, heading down the footpath. 'I know your mother enjoyed going away for holidays, but Ned doesn't like the bright lights.'

'You've really wormed your way in there, haven't you?'

Pain stilled her as she fixed her gaze on the plate glass windows of the café. 'I thought we were going to talk about the practice.'

She could see Morgan's tall figure behind her in the glass. He made her feel small. Once upon a time that had included feeling protected. She'd loved him for that, even without all the other things.

He sighed, with a lift of his shoulders she could see against the background of the trees and the shops across the street. 'I'm sorry. We better go in.'

They settled in a booth against one wall under a series of paintings depicting rural scenes with small price tags fixed to one corner of the frames.

She ordered a slice of quiche and bottled water from the young waitress who was clearly intrigued by the appearance of Morgan, an apparent stranger in the small town. Morgan took longer, scanning the menu with its kitschy illustrations of food with slightly raised brows.

'I'll have the gourmet meat pie with sweet potato fries and aioli sauce.'

When the girl had gone, Becca studied Morgan. 'Taking your mother's criticism to heart?'

'I wasn't aware you were privy to my mother's concerns about my weight.'

'Half the town is aware your mother has been worried about you.'

'I suppose nothing much has changed with the grapevine.'

Becca shrugged. 'It's not as efficient as it used to be. There are quite a lot of new people in town. They haven't divulged all their secrets yet.'

'Much to Beryl Harmsworth's disappointment I'm sure.'

His crooked smile did something strange to her heart and she focused her attention on the bottle of local spring water delivered by the waitress. She didn't know how people coped with seeing their ex-lovers around town. Bad enough to remember the emotional response to the breakup without having flashbacks of getting naked with them. Heat flushed over her skin, zipping along nerve endings and she pressed her knees together, hating that her body was so out of control.

Think about work. That's why they were here. 'Tell me about your plans. For the practice.' He'd looked odd when she'd asked the question and she hastily added the disclaimer.

Leaning forward in his chair, elbows on the table, Morgan studied the nearby tables. There was no-one close but he kept his voice low. 'I'm thinking of expanding. Bringing in more doctors and another practice nurse. There's room to put a small day surgery in the large unused area at the back. Ultrasound and colonoscopies. Antenatal clinics. A mental health unit. Small procedures. It would save people travelling to Bialga.'

'Is there the population here?'

'I was talking to the nursing superintendent at the hospital and the visiting surgeon, Michael Long, and they both think so. The town is growing fast and Doc Farrell couldn't cope with the growth. He should have brought in a partner or two instead of trying to keep up with locums coming and going. The overflow has to go out of town. It would help keep business in the town. If people travel to Bialga for appointments, they tend to shop there too.'

Becca wondered what all these changes would mean for the local staff. For her. 'I suppose you'd want someone with more experience in a large practice to do the management.'

'Don't you think you're up to it?'

It sounded like a challenge and she nodded. 'Of course I am. But you hardly know enough about my skills to have confidence in me for an expansion like the one you're talking about.'

'It's not going to happen overnight. There'll be more administration staff needed to handle the increased load. Another receptionist perhaps and someone in the back office.'

'Do you plan to settle here?'

Morgan straightened as the waitress placed the food on the table. He watched her go to another customer before he spoke. 'I'm planning on three years to start with. A lot will depend on my parents' health. If I have partners, it won't be such a disruption if I go away again.'

Becca faced her quiche with a vastly reduced appetite. She forced it down, mouthful by mouthful, but she couldn't find words for idle chitchat over the meal. Morgan seemed to have lost his desire to eat as well, poking at the pie with his fork and eating the chips with his free hand, dunking them in the generous dollop of aioli.

'I met your children yesterday.'

Becca dropped her fork with a clatter onto the plate. She'd had Gabby telling her all about Morgan over the dinner table and her sly looks and leading questions had given away her line of thought. If Morgan had come to the same conclusion...

'You were at your parents place after you left work?'

'Yes.' He placed the cutlery neatly on the plate beside his half-finished food. 'Could you explain how my parents came to be your babysitters?'

The air left her lungs with a woosh that must be obvious to the man watching her so closely. Not the question she was expecting, but a difficult one all the same. 'I got to know them better after you left. The last time. After the ... accident. I did them a favour and they offered to help with the babysitting. My mother hadn't long passed away and Aunt Bea was in Brisbane with Dan while he was in rehab.'

'I'm sorry about your mother.'

'It was a relief in the end.'

He glanced around the room again before pushing his plate away. 'My parents know about Gabby, don't they?'

Becca quelled the nausea that sent bile to the back of her throat. 'I can't say.'

'Look, Becca, I'm not trying to cause trouble in your family. There are reasons...' He rested his forearms on the table. 'I'd like to get to know her.'

The room didn't have enough oxygen. She sucked in a hoarse breath and stood. 'I have to go outside.' She fumbled in her bag for a twenty dollar note and tossed it on the table. 'I'm sorry.'

***

Morgan found her at the other end of the block, staring at the bridge over the creek. The sign behind her said Maiden's Bridge, Redemption Creek and it seemed strangely apt. Her arms were wrapped tightly around her body, the posture defensive. The vulnerability stirred an uneasy sensation in his gut, reminding him of the first time he met her properly, hiding in the shed at the back of the Maiden place. He'd been playing cricket with the guys and they'd wanted a haybale to stand in as a wicket because Ben had left his set at home.

She must have been about six or seven to his ten years and he'd crouched down to talk to her. He knew who she was because he'd seen her waiting for the school bus with Dan often enough. It was summer holidays and she was wearing an old hand-me-down boys t-shirt and shorts. Her left arm was badly bruised and he reached out to take her hand to get a better look. She'd flinched away and he'd spoken softly, gentling her like a wounded puppy.

She'd told him a long, convoluted story about falling down the steps at home. Not surprising considering how narrow and rickety they were. Dan had confirmed it when he turned up to see why he'd taken so long. 'She's always taking a tumble. Little idiot.'

Years later, he'd wondered if her proneness to accidents had something to do with her alcoholic stepfather but after his death, she'd still occasionally turned up with the same bumps and bruises.

Dan had been typically dismissive of her, not interested in someone who was almost like a younger sibling and a girl as well. He'd been annoyed and embarrassed when she started hanging around their group. Not participating, but often watching their games or perched on a rock by the river watching them swim. Morgan wondered exactly when Dan's attitude to his step-cousin changed.

'Becca?'

She hunched her shoulders and he couldn't tell if she was feeling the cold or rejecting him. Probably both.

'I told you I don't want to stir things up. It shouldn't be hard for me to spend time with Gabby if she's at my parents' place.'

She looked up warily. 'Only Gabby?'

There was a thread of something in her tone that sounded like disapproval.

'Obviously if Edward is there too, I'll spend time with them both. But Gabby...'

'Gabby looks like you and Edward looks like me. I suppose I can understand that. You wouldn't want to be reminded of me and the mistake you made, would you?'

She had it all wrong, but she'd marched away, turning up the street that ran along the park overlooking the creek before he could explain. Why would she be offended because he didn't want to spend time with her other child? He'd have expected she'd want to keep him out of it. With a sudden clarity, he realised she hadn't agreed to anything. Hadn't agreed to him seeing Gabby.

He followed her the length of the block and turned back towards the main street as she was entering the clinic. By the time he caught up with her, she was already shedding her coat in the staff room and talking with Karen about the afternoon schedule. There wasn't any point in hanging around. She'd be busy until the end of her shift and he had an appointment he had to keep.

*

'This is going to cost you a packet, Morgan. I hope they've been paying you well.'

Morgan remembered Mike Maloney from school. He'd done his apprenticeship in Bialga but came home to set up his electrical contracting business. They'd never been friends, but there was an old camaraderie of remembered school days.

Morgan shrugged. 'Nothing to spend it on where I've been so I've accumulated enough to fix up this place.' And purchase the medical practice outright without a loan. They'd been empty years on the personal front, but productive for his career and investments.

He followed the electrician to the back door and around the house, the front steps being too dangerous for casual use. The carpenter would be coming tomorrow to assess the major jobs Morgan didn't feel confident doing himself. 'I need it made safe and it's an investment.'

Mike glanced around at the property. 'The house is great. It should do up nicely. It's solid enough and once you upgrade the plumbing and electricals, it'll be liveable. Most of the damage is peripheral because of the neglect. A coat of paint will make all the difference.'

Morgan let the words flow over him, watching the two children pedalling up his parents' driveway. He couldn't crash their homework time again. There was still the issue of his parents' knowledge about Gabby he needed to deal with.

He'd been too shell-shocked at the revelations to speak to them last night. Still angry at what he'd been denied to bring up the subject over the meal. He'd made himself scarce when Becca came to pick them up but he'd watched from his parents' front bedroom as they did the short trip to the battered old house across the dirt road.

He'd never in his wildest dreams imagined he'd have a child, a daughter. Not once the physical and mental aftermath of the night nearly thirteen years ago had manifested itself. His life had changed in ways he couldn't have imagined, though it had taken months before he'd been forced to acknowledge he had a problem and then years to come to grips with managing his condition. He'd barely stabilised when his more recent illness had started the whole thing over again. The specialist had been hopeful, but Morgan was not.

Mike paused before climbing into his truck, his gaze following Morgan's to the children entering his parents' place. 'It would make a great family home.'

It was a relief when he didn't wait for an answer, rumbling down the bumpy driveway with a wave of the hand as he turned onto the road.

Morgan turned to look at the house. A family home.

Mike was right. It had a multitude of bedrooms and larger rooms for entertaining or family recreation. All of it surrounded by wide verandahs with carved finials and balustrades. Underneath had been enclosed with brick against the cold winters and with the old-fashioned central heating, it was easy to keep warm. It had been a magnificent homestead in its day, the original owner's wealthy beyond imagination and ruling the upper echelons of the town's citizenry long before the Smith and Cavanaugh families arrived at Maiden's Landing. They'd been the original squattocracy, owning most of the district until it had been cut up by succeeding generations and the town established.

He made his way carefully up the front steps, avoiding the ones too damaged to bear his weight. The view was worth every cent he'd paid, overlooking the river and beyond it to the west he could see the town itself. The post office tower helped him pinpoint the centre of town. He could see Becca's house down in the hollow, beside the river, surrounded by pine trees and natives. They'd been small, newly planted the last time he'd been here, the house itself an eyesore surrounded by rusty cars and farm machinery. These days the yard was bare apart from the trees and a small vegetable garden to one side. Becca's doing, or Dan's?

His hand was on the front door when a shout caught his attention and he twisted his head to see Gabby running across the paddock, still in her winter school uniform of green polo shirt and matching tracksuit pants.

'Morgan?'

The boy was following at a slower pace, a green environmental shopping bag in one hand.

Gabby had one foot on the bottom step when he stopped her with a sharp word. His heart tightened at the sudden wiping of the smile from her face.

'It's okay to be here, but the steps aren't safe. You need to come around to the back porch.'

The sun-bright smile beamed up at him. 'We'll meet you there.'

He went through the house to let them in the back door and he could hear them arguing. Edward wasn't happy. 'We shouldn't be here. Mum won't like it.'

'We have permission from Grace and Grandpa Ned. We're doing a job for them.'

Morgan opened the door and Gabby tumbled into the small room that had served as a dumping ground for shoes and coats back when he came here as a child.

'What brings you here? Have you done your homework?'

'There wasn't much.' Gabby drew her reluctant brother inside. 'Grace sent over some baking for you. Your favourites.'

Edward held up the bag and Morgan took it. 'Thanks. Did you want to come in?'

Gabby danced passed him into the kitchen. 'We were hoping you'd invite us for afternoon tea.'

She looked around curiously and he revisited the dingy room through her youthful eyes.

'I haven't started the renovations yet.'

Making herself comfortable at the old Laminex table, Gabby nodded. 'It's like ours. Mum wants to fix it up but she can't afford it. You don't have to worry about impressing us you know.'

Morgan smiled back at her. 'I suppose it's the food that's the important thing.'

Delving into the bag, he pulled out the Tupperware containers and stacked them on the table. Anzac biscuits, some choc chip cookies and a chocolate cake. He wondered if it had been Grace's idea to send the children or his father's.

'What would you like?'

Gabby glanced across at her brother. 'Edward likes chocolate cake. Anyway, it doesn't keep as well as biscuits so you should eat it first.'

Edward's cheeks flushed a dull red. 'Mum says you should take what you're given.'

A kindred feeling swept through Morgan at the reserved boy's obvious discomfort at his sister's forwardness. He'd been much the same at his age, taking a while to get comfortable with strangers. 'Come and sit at the table, Edward. What would you like to drink?'

The boy hesitated and Morgan went to the fridge. 'I have apple juice and prune juice or milk.'

Gabby wrinkled up her nose. 'Prunes? Yuck. I'll have apple.'

'Me too,' came Edward's small voice.

It was fun spending the time with the kids. Edward relaxed under the influence of chocolate cake and joined in the banter. Morgan found he liked both of them in their different ways. He'd thought Gabby might overwhelm her brother but when he spoke, she listened with grave attention. At least he was learning more about the town as they talked about their schoolteachers and various people, some of whom were familiar and some not.

They were laughing over Gabby's imitation of Miss Harmsworth when Edward suddenly stopped, his mouth slamming shut, eyes fixed on the doorway.

It was hard to read Becca's expression. She'd developed a real talent for putting on a mask to hide her thoughts. But then she'd always kept secrets. He glanced at Gabby. Still did.

Gabby twisted around, her smile a little shaky. 'Hi, Mum.'

'Hello.' She stepped into the kitchen wearing jeans and a hoodie and holding a sweater over one arm. After a quick glance at the food on the table she nodded in Morgan's direction. 'Thanks for having them.'

Morgan stood and indicated a spare seat. 'Please join us.'

Something flickered in her dark eyes behind the spectacles. 'We need to get home. Dan will be waiting.'

'Aw, Mum.' Gabby looked like she might argue, but Edward was already standing, wiping the cake crumbs from around his mouth.

Morgan forced himself to smile at Gabby. He'd forgotten about Dan for the moment. 'Another time. You know you're always welcome.'

Becca handed her daughter the sweater. 'You forgot this and it's cold outside. Both of you head off and pick up your school bags and bikes. I'll be along in a few minutes.'

Both children had a worried notch between their brows, but they obeyed, giving a wave to Morgan as they went through the back porch.

Becca was silent as she watched them leave. He had a feeling he wasn't going to like this conversation.

'Whose idea was it for them to come here?'

Morgan perched on the edge of the table. 'I presume it was Gabby. They were doing a small job for my mother.'

Her gaze drifted again to the table. 'Grace has been cooking up a storm.'

'Trying to fatten me up.'

A small twitch at the corner of her mouth was all the response he received, but he relaxed.

'Is there any reason why the children can't come for a visit?'

'Why would you want them?'

'They're nice kids. You've done a great job with them, you and Dan,' he added.

A flush highlighted her cheekbones. 'They are good kids. I wouldn't be without them.' It came out almost defiantly and he wondered who had made her so defensive. And why.

She was fiddling with the cords at the neck of her hoodie. 'I expected you would have been married. Have your own family.'

'I'm not much good to a woman, to be honest.'

With a frown, she scanned him top to bottom and back again. 'Because you've been sick? Is there something permanent? Will you recover fully?'

'I'd almost think you cared.' A touch of the old bitterness put an edge on his words and he sucked in a deep breath. He wasn't going to let her think he was still carrying scars from all that time ago.

'Don't be ridiculous. It's only natural I care if you're sick. I've known you most of my life.'

Which put him effectively in his place.

'Much appreciated.'

'I don't want to fight with you, Morgan. I've been thinking about what you asked today. It looks pretty pointless trying to forbid them to come and visit and you'll be seeing them around. I'm all right with you spending time with them, but it has to be fair. If Edward wants to join you and Gabby, he needs to feel welcome.'

'I wouldn't do anything to hurt him, Becca. I like him.'

'Good.' With an air of finality she moved towards the door.

'One question, Becca.'

Her brows drew together over the narrow frames. 'Yes?'

'Did my parents know?'

Her eyes closed as she breathed deep, her shoulders rising and falling. 'You need to talk to them about it.'

'Is that a yes?'

A bleakness shadowed her eyes under the glint of glass. 'Ask them.'

And she was gone, slipping out into the twilight leaving more questions unanswered than the spoken ones.

Chapter 5

Becca piled the containers of sandwiches onto the table in the school tuckshop and waved off the twins. They scooted off to the playground, heading for a group of their friends. Most of the kids were younger, even though it was a P-12 school covering all the grades. High school aged kids probably didn't want to hang around school on a weekend and were old enough to be left while their parents came.

'They're getting tall.' Marcia from the Hot Bread Shop brushed her hands off on a tea towel.

Becca watched them greet their friends with an enthusiasm that suggested they hadn't seen them for months, instead of yesterday. But they didn't usually get to see them on the weekend. 'They'll be grown up before I know it.'

Marcia wrinkled her nose. 'Don't say that. I'm feeling old at the moment.'

Becca turned to look at her, envious of the curves and the retro style that made the most of her shape. 'I forgot it was your birthday this month. The twins will be twelve. Talk about feeling old.'

Marcia's beautifully made-up mouth curved up at one corner. 'It happens to us all. Sorry, I have to fly. Things to do, people to see. Hope the working bee goes okay.'

Eyeing the large supply of cupcakes, all beautifully decorated, Becca nodded. 'They'll be well fed. Thanks for this.' Marcia didn't have children at the school, but she always seemed to be donating her cupcakes to events.

'Someone can drop the containers back to the shop on Monday.' Marcia darted out of the tuckshop, making her way past a group of fathers who paused in their digging to watch her go by.

A tall figure with red hair near the gate caught Becca's attention. Surely Morgan wouldn't be coming to a school working bee. She paused in sorting through the box of paper serviettes to watch the new arrivals. It was Morgan, talking with Sabine Mallings, one of the schoolteachers. Another local girl so Morgan probably remembered her, though she was younger than Becca by a couple of years. They looked good together, the tall elegant blonde and Morgan.

He was looking better every day, filling out and losing the dark shadows under his eyes. In a white tee and jeans and a leather bomber jacket it reminded her of how he'd dressed back in the day. He hadn't filled out as much at nineteen, but the height was already there.

'Do you think they're an item?'

Becca jerked her attention back to her task, hoping Celie hadn't spotted her drooling. In her absorption with Morgan, she hadn't noticed the other mother approach. She was nice, but her children were younger so Becca didn't have much to do with her apart from these events. 'I wouldn't know. He's only been back a week or so.'

Celie seemed indifferent. 'It's early days, I guess.'

Grateful the other woman wasn't a long-time resident and couldn't know the history, Becca shrugged and set out the napkins in piles. 'Do you think this will be enough?'

Casting a critical eye over the supplies, Celie nodded. 'Should be. It's a good turnout, but most of them will go home at lunchtime.'

There was no more time for conversation as the workers started coming over, seeking drinks and eats. Celie manned the hot water urn supplying tea and coffee while Becca focused on distributing the food, all the while keeping half an eye on Morgan and his female friend.

She wasn't jealous. It was worry that churned her stomach and tightened her throat.

Now Morgan was home, so many things were changing. Her cosy little world was under threat.

She almost forgot Morgan in the rush of dealing with the multitude of children all chasing Marcia's cupcakes and directing them to the water fountains for drinks. Her own children had swooped down and possessed themselves of more than their fair share of the cakes and run off before she could confiscate the surplus.

He appeared at the tuckshop window while she was handing Celie's youngest the last of the pink cupcakes. Her heart went all *pittapat* at the sight of him looking sweaty and tired, putting on his jacket against the chill of the air.

'You've overdone it.'

He used a handkerchief to mop his face and tucked it into his jacket pocket. 'I need to do physical work or I won't get fit.'

Celie offered him a cup of tea and he took it with a smile that sent Becca's heart into overdrive.

'I don't think we've met. I'm Celie, Lucille Taite.'

Morgan put down the tea and gripped her extended hand. 'Would you be married to Jordan Taite? He's a cousin on my mother's side.'

Celie nodded. 'Eight years ago.'

'Family?'

'Three children.'

Morgan blinked. 'Hard to imagine Jordan embracing parenthood so enthusiastically. I'm sorry we haven't met. One of the perils of leaving the country. Is he still as ambitious as ever?'

'That's him.' Celie's smile wobbled. 'No doubt we'll be seeing more of you. The whole family seem to be disaster prone at the moment.'

Morgan murmured something Celie responded to with a smile. Gathering her things together, she waved as she took her leave of them both. 'I need to find the kids and get them home. You should be able to cope, Becca. Looks like the rush is over for now.'

With a wry smile, Morgan took up his tea and a cupcake. 'The joy of small towns. I suppose I'll get to know the new faces fast enough. Do you think I upset her when I said I was surprised about Jordan having kids?'

'No. They're having a tough time on the farm since his parents died, that's all.'

He frowned after Celie. 'I should have mentioned how sorry I was to hear about their loss. She's not a local girl?'

'No. She went to school with Jordan's sister in Brisbane.'

'Susannah? I remember her as being pretty but consumed with boys.'

'She's married.' It came out in a snap and Becca hoped Morgan didn't put it down to jealousy.

She wasn't jealous. He could admire all the women he liked. Date them if he wanted. As long as he didn't disrupt her carefully planned life with the twins. Although it might be too late to stop that happening.

He didn't say anything, blowing gently on his tea, but his raised brows indicated he was surprised at her response. In an effort to keep her distance, Becca focused on the people beyond him and recognised the blonde schoolteacher rounding up a group of kindergarteners.

'I didn't know you were friends with Sabine?' Oh great. Now she was showing off her jealousy in another direction.

'Jealousy?' Morgan hesitated with the last of a bright purple cupcake at his lips. 'Who's jealous? Of who?'

She was thinking out loud now? Becca glared at the school gate, wondering if she could make a break for it.

She fiddled with the tray of cupcakes, arranging them in lines of individual colours and then had to figure out where to put the solitary rainbow decorated one. The vibrant design had been one of the most popular with both the girls and the boys.

'Becca?'

'All right, it was me. Not now, but at high school. You remember what an outsider I was.

Sabine used to be in the cool group. All the popular girls. It's not a big school so they came from different classes and sat together at lunchtime. I think they did ballet together after school. Sabine and Brittany and a couple of other girls. All rich and pretty and with boys drooling all over them. I'd almost forgotten.'

'You wanted to be drooled all over? Or do ballet?'

'Yuck, no. The guys were jerks anyway. Most of them.'

Morgan grinned. 'You liked one of them.'

'Of course not.' His speculative look disturbed her and she hoped he didn't remember her crush on him. It had started long before he took any notice of her. How embarrassing to be stuck on one guy your whole life. She could sense heat rising up her throat, warming her cheeks. 'Maybe one or two. Andrew Maiden was nice. You'd remember him. He was the one in Dan's class.'

'Where is Dan? I expected him to be here for the working bee.'

'He works at the organic farm with Thackery on the weekend.'

'In Bialga all week and on the farm on the weekend. You mustn't see much of each other.'

'He's usually home for tea.'

Morgan placed his cup on the bench with the other discards. 'You said you used to be jealous. But you aren't now?'

Becca started stacking the cups. 'Why should I be? I've got everything I need. Besides...'

'Besides...?'

'Look what happened to them. I thought they had a charmed life and poor Brittany died at sixteen and Sabine...'

She stumbled to a halt and heat washed up her cheeks again.

'What about Sabine?'

'She was injured in a car crash. A few years after Dan and Brittany's accident. A drunk hit her and her boyfriend on the bridge and they all ended up in the river.'

Morgan scanned the crowd for Sabine. 'She looks great now.'

'Yes, they were pulled out quickly. The drunk driver was killed. He drowned.'

'What happened to the boyfriend?'

'He went back to university. I don't know what happened afterwards. I understand he went overseas.'

'Is she with anyone at the moment? Husband, boyfriend?'

With a quick lift of the chin to hide the pain, Becca focused on his face. 'Are you interested?'

'Maybe. Does she teach primary or high?'

'High. She also does tutoring after school.'

With what seemed like an effort, he dragged his gaze back from the attractive teacher. If Morgan was going to use her as a dating app it was going to be far too painful. 'She rarely dates, so you have an open field.'

'Thanks.' It was said almost absently. 'I'll catch you later. I want to talk to you about Gabby.'

***

Morgan headed for the playing fields to let Gabby know he'd kept his promise to come, but found he was caught up with conversations with people who'd known him years ago. It was gratifying how many people remembered him, considering he'd hardly been back since he graduated from grade ten and went away to boarding school for the last couple of school years.

Some he'd had a refresher with at the surgery since he'd come back, but quite a few remembered him from school. It was the right age group, most of them with young families. He could have had all those things too, if things hadn't gone pear shaped with Becca. Now it was unlikely to ever happen.

A shriek from the playground pulled him away from a conversation with a girl from his class at primary school whose name escaped him. She turned to scan the children.

'It's Gabby Walters. Not one of mine, thankfully.'

'Gabby?' Morgan muttered a hasty excuse and sprinted across to the group gathered by the climbing frame, his heart pounding from more than the exercise.

Gabby was surrounded by the time he got there and he shouldered his way through. 'I'm a doctor.'

She was sprawled under the flying fox with a fresh cut on one cheek and a dazed look in her eyes. 'Morgan? You came.' Her smile squeezed his heart.

'Of course I came. Someone has to patch you up when you find out you don't have wings.'

Stretching her arms out she looked at them. 'I don't? That's disappointing.'

He examined her swiftly while Sabine shunted the rest of the children away. 'We might have to put a Band-Aid or two on some of these scrapes.'

Sabine turned back as she guided one particularly curious child away. 'The first aid kit is in the room behind the tuckshop.'

Scooping up Gabby, Morgan carried her back to the school building, aiming for the tuckshop. He needed to let Becca know what was happening.

For a moment he thought she wasn't there, but the clatter of dishes told him where she was. 'Becca?'

She poked her head out of the large pantry. Her eyes widened as she recognised Gabby. 'Are you hurt?'

'Just a bump and some scrapes.'

Gabby wriggled in his hold. 'I'm okay. Morgan's going to put on a Band-Aid.'

Becca seemed lost for a moment and a flash of resentment came and went on her normally unreadable face as she silently acknowledged Gabby's preference. 'If you're sure you're okay, I'll keep going here and then find Edward. It's pretty much done for today.'

Morgan nodded, glancing around at the rapidly emptying school yard. Most people seemed to be going home as there'd been enough parents working to finish the project.

The first aid room was well-equipped and it only took a moment for Morgan to find what he needed and start cleaning up the scrapes on her hands. Fortunately, her jeans and long-sleeved pullover had protected her knees and elbows from receiving more than a few bruises.

'I hate being clumsy.'

Morgan lifted her onto his lap. 'It's okay. I remember your mother was always covered in bruises when she was a child. She seemed to bump into something or trip down the steps regularly.' An unease shifted something in his gut. 'I remember the last time I saw her she had a bruise on her cheek. From running into the door of one of the kitchen cupboards. That's what she told me, anyway.'

Sharp as a photograph he remembered the scene. Dan standing by the sink and Becca rummaging in the freezer for an icepack, hair dishevelled and the buttons on her top undone. He'd walked in unexpectedly and the two had split apart as if they had something to hide. Becca had mumbled something about her step-cousin checking her eye for damage but the smirk on Dan's face had made her out a liar. All the hints Dan had been trickling in his ear for months had coalesced and he'd known there was something more between them than simply being step-cousins. The moment Becca had left the room to get changed, Dan had been in his ear. He shouldn't have listened. Shouldn't have acted on the vicious words that had broken something inside him. Because of that, he'd lost Gabby. Lost everything. Lost Becca.

Gabby dabbed her cheek with a sterile dressing pad, examining the blood with a ghoulish interest. 'Aunt Bea said Mummy wasn't nearly as clumsy since Dan had his accident.'

'Aunt Bea?'

'You know, Dan's mum. She died a couple of years ago. She got cancer the same as Nanna. Miss Harmsworth says they smoked themselves to death.'

'Miss Harmsworth should mind her own business.'

'That's what Mummy says. All. The. Time.'

The signature eye roll was back and Morgan gave her a gentle shove off his knees. 'You should be good to go now. Run next door and check in with your mother.'

He watched her limp across to the tuckshop where Edward was waiting, eating a bright green cupcake. The lad handed a blue one to Gabby who wolfed it down with the appetite of the young. She was bouncing back quickly.

Morgan didn't feel quite so carefree. He'd had a sudden insight into the past and he didn't like what he was seeing.

**

Gathering her containers together, Becca distributed some of them between the twins and picked up the rest. The day was only half done and she was exhausted. At least she wouldn't have to deal with Dan until late. Thackery usually kept him there for the evening, giving him a meal and watching Dan's favourite action movies. It meant Becca and the children had one evening where they had family time alone. It wasn't easy for the kids having to deal with Dan, though he was a much nicer person these days.

Almost everyone else was gone by the time they reached the carpark. Morgan was there, doing the gentlemanly thing and opening the door of his car for Sabine. It was a nice car, an upmarket four-wheel-drive ideal for the rural roads, some of which were pretty rough when they headed into the hills. It was better to think about that than wonder why he'd been the one to take the pretty teacher home from the working bee. Especially as Sabine's house was only a couple of blocks from the school.

She was focused on putting the food containers into the carriers on the bikes when Morgan suddenly appeared at her side.

'Do you need a hand with those?'

He was way too close. 'We've got the extra ones to be returned to Marcia's on Monday, so I'm having a problem fitting them in.'

'I'll take them. Pop them in the boot and I'll drop yours home later and bring the rest into work on Monday.'

The transfer took place under Sabine's interested gaze. Becca wondered if the speculative look she was giving Gabby and Morgan meant she was figuring out the connection. There had been a few curious looks from other parents. Especially when Morgan had carried Gabby after the accident. The whole town would have it figured out before long if Morgan didn't hold his distance. There'd been curiosity when they'd first been born of course, but it had largely faded as the years had gone by without Morgan returning. At least the gossip had.

Maybe it was a good thing he seemed interested in Sabine. At least she was a nice person so if it got serious...

Becca shuddered. She didn't want to think about Morgan getting married. It would make his wife stepmother to the twins.

And leave you on the outside, a cold voice whispered insidiously.

She waved the twins to go ahead so she could follow and keep an eye on them. She'd always been on the outside, so it was nothing new. Except with the twins, and Morgan was threatening that closeness. The moment when she'd realised Gabby preferred Morgan to mend her wounds had come as a shock. The twins had always come to her before. Now Gabby had moved some of her allegiance to Morgan. As it should be. It didn't make it any easier to live with.

Morgan arrived late afternoon when Becca was alone in the garden. She was grateful she'd put on a nice pair of jeans and a pullover without holes in the elbows. There had been a moment when she'd picked up the tatty faded clothes she usually wore in the garden, but knowing Morgan might turn up had her looking for something nicer, without being too obvious. He'd apparently enjoyed his lunch with Sabine if he hadn't come home until now.

The pain in her chest pinched and she sucked in a breath to ease it as Morgan came through the rusty gate, carefully closing it again. She winced at the protesting noise of metal against metal from the hinges.

'You should probably get the gate seen to. The neighbours are going to think you're murdering someone.'

Brushing her gloved hands on her jeans, Becca raised an eyebrow. She wasn't going to mention the family used the larger driveway gate. Visitors using the footpath were few and far between. 'One of the advantages of living out of town. Most neighbours are too far away to notice.'

They'd certainly never indicated they'd been aware of any suspicious noises in the past.

Thumbs in his pockets, Morgan wandered further into the vegetable patch. 'You've got a lot of things still growing well for this time of year. Broccoli, brussels sprouts, silver beet. What's that one?'

'Kale.'

'Plus rhubarb. Do you still make the German rhubarb cake I liked?'

'For special occasions. I tend to cook biscuits mostly. They're easier for school lunches.' She wished he'd get on with things. 'I'm assuming you're here to return the containers?'

'I thought I might check on Gabby too. How is she?'

'I think she's still asleep. She went for a lie down after lunch and dropped off.'

'No concussion?'

'I checked on her a couple of times. She was tired and sore, but no headache.'

'Good.'

He still seemed reluctant to move, staring down at the trees partially obscuring the river and the fancy house on the far side.

'I'm sure you have places you need to be. I'll come and get the containers and you can head off.'

'No hurry.' He turned slowly in place, his gaze directed up at his new home and his parents' place. 'Mum and Dad are having dinner with some friends at the bistro, so I'm at a loose end.'

Which sounded like a hint, but she wasn't playing. 'Lucky you. A chance to catch up with some old friends.'

'Good idea. How about I join you for dinner? We could do some catching up. I haven't seen Dan yet.'

'He won't be home until late.'

'Still the same old party animal. Why aren't you with him? No babysitter?'

'Are you offering?'

'By all means. I suppose normally my parents babysit when you go out on the town.'

Fat chance. 'Dan is with Thackery. I usually stay with the children when he's out. We play board games and watch kid's movies. It's family time.'

She wished she hadn't added the last bit when his brows drew together in a frown. He was family. 'If you want, you can stay. But it's only pizza.'

'Pizza sounds great.' He actually looked excited, his pale eyes brightening. 'So, what is it tonight, board games or movie?'

'Scrabble.'

His grin broadened, showing his perfectly straight teeth courtesy of the best orthodontist in Bialga. It always made her conscious of the slight crookedness of her own teeth.

'So, you finish here in the garden while I bring in your containers.'

'Do you know which ones?'

'The cupcake ones are all labelled. Since when do we have a Hot Bread Shop?'

'About three years. A lot of new shops opened up along the creek when we became a bona fide tourist destination.'

'Near the park?'

'Mostly. A few in the main drag down the other end close to the bridge.'

'I'll have to do a tour. Do you want to be my guide?'

Her look must have said everything because he only smiled and headed for the car. She watched him go, liking the easy lope as his long legs covered the ground quickly. Before he reached the car, she turned back to her task, trimming some silver beet leaves for the pizza.

Chapter 6

It had been close to thirteen years since Morgan had last entered Becca's home. The old caravan behind the house that had been home to Dan and his mother was gone. He'd been to a few parties there with Dan, but once they included drugs, he'd backed off. By then he preferred to spend his time with Becca anyway, usually at his place.

The stairs up to the back door were still wobbly. A brick was placed under one end of the bottom step to replace the rotted timber. Carefully balancing the plastic containers, he opened the door and stepped into the kitchen closing the door behind him.

A muffled sob sent him spinning and he almost lost the containers, managing to dump them on the table before they scattered. A brown dog shot out from under the nearest chair, ears flattened, and vanished through the doggy door and down the back stairs.

Edward was seated at the far end of the old Laminex table, hastily wiping tears from flushed cheeks. 'What are you doing here?'

Morgan ignored the belligerent tone and straightened the pile of containers. 'Dropping these off. I wanted to see Gabby too.'

'She's asleep.'

'Your mum said it's okay to go check on her.'

His slight shoulders hunched as he kept his face averted. 'Through the hall, second on the right.'

Leaving the boy to recover himself, Morgan entered the hall, passing the bathroom and a closed door on the left. There were photographs on the walls, not professional portraits. Grouped casual shots of the children, separately and together, in cheap frames. He dragged himself away, promising himself a better look another time.

Gabby must share with her brother, if the twin beds and airplane models hanging from the ceiling and ships and cars on the desk were any indication. Gabby was under her bright pink and purple doona, her red hair loose on the pillow. The mark on her cheek was turning into a bruise but it had stopped bleeding. He did the usual checks for concussion, disturbing her briefly, but she turned away with a mutter when he'd thought she might wake up.

He knew there were three bedrooms, so it surprised him the children still shared. Not his business but it explained why Edward was doing his model building on the kitchen table today. With a last look at the sleeping girl, he went back to the kitchen, intending to re-join Becca in the garden.

'Mum said you're staying for dinner.'

Morgan hesitated, unsure whether to engage with the boy. He must have been outside to speak to his mother. His hair was slightly damp at the front, indicating he'd had a quick wash to remove the evidence of his tears. 'Is it all right with you?'

'Yeah. It's cool.'

'What are you making?'

'The *Santa Maria.*'

Morgan shifted so he could see the partially built model in a better light. 'Isn't the *Santa Maria* the one Columbus sailed in to discover America?'

The boy's brown eyes brightened. 'Yes. I have a kit for *La Pinta* and Mum promised me *Endeavour* for my birthday. It was Captain Cook's ship.'

'It looks tricky.'

'Sailing ships are hard, because of the rigging. It's fiddly.'

Without realising it, Morgan found himself drawn in, listening to the boy expound on the ship and holding bits and pieces for him, helping with the strings and sails.

Edward gazed up at him with a glow in his eyes reminiscent of Becca's long ago warm appreciation. 'How come you're so good with knots?'

'I have to tie tiny stitches as part of my job.'

'Oooh yuck. I don't think I could be a doctor. Blood and stuff. I prefer making things. I might be an engineer when I grow up.'

'An engineer sounds like a great job.'

Packing away his tools, Edward nodded. 'Mum said I could travel all over the world building things.'

'You'd like to travel?'

'Yeah. You've travelled, haven't you? I remember you telling Gabby.'

'Mostly with my job. My boss in Brisbane came from Africa and I went with him when he went home to Rwanda to train doctors in his home country. I worked there mostly, but I went to the USA for some conferences and did a locum in Britain for six months.'

'Didn't you miss your mum and dad?'

'We emailed a lot.'

'I love Grandpa Ned. He likes building things too. Grace thinks Gabby should do cooking with her but she likes to be outside. I don't mind cooking. It's kind of like making things, isn't it?'

'Except you get to eat it.' Morgan noted and wasn't surprised by the intimacy with his father but was surprised by his mother allowing such familiarity. 'Why do you call Grace by her first name?'

'Mum always called her Grace, so we started to when we were small. Mum said we should call her Mrs Cavanaugh but Grandpa Ned said it was too tricky for littlies. Grace told Mum she didn't feel it right to be called Aunty Grace and it would be hyp-hypocritical to be called Grandmother.' He paused, the glue bottle in one hand. 'Why would it be hypocritical? I thought old ladies liked to be grandmothers.'

Morgan almost laughed at the thought of his mother revelling in being a grandmother. She wanted grandchildren, but not the implication of age. Perhaps because she'd been an older mother when he'd been born.

A shiver of something under his feet alerted Morgan to someone on the back steps. The whole house probably needed restumping, but it was hardly worth it. If Becca ever sold it, the house would be bulldozed and a fancy waterfront mansion would take its place. Most of the privately-owned land along the river had been subdivided into acreage allotments and lush new houses built. It was surprising she hadn't sold it, unless Dan had a stake in it.

He stood as the back door opened and Becca paused at the top of the steps, her eyes wary. An old cane basket hung off one arm with a few silver beet leaves hanging over the edge.

Morgan stared back at her, trying to read her face. He missed being able to. The younger Becca had been easier to figure out, only clamming up when her family was mentioned.

Edward pushed his chair back with a scraping sound. 'I've finished the ship. Morgan helped me.'

Her stiffness melted away as she smiled at her son. 'Finally. I thought you were never going to get it done.'

'I'll start on *La Pinta* next. Can you help again, Morgan?' He peeked up shyly, the look in his eyes expecting rejection. Where was Dan when he was needed? The boy was crying out for a father's interest.

'I'll have to see. Things can get busy at the surgery.'

The resigned expression on his young face smote at Morgan's heart. 'I'm sure I can make time. Even doctors get days off.'

He looked up, shocked to see Becca's face drawn in pain. She carefully smoothed out the lines of strain and fixed a smile on her mouth as she put the basket on the sink. 'You don't have to.'

'I enjoyed it. I used to make models when I was about his age.'

Edward nodded, his smile wide. 'Grandpa Ned showed me. Airplanes.' He hesitated. 'A couple of the ones in my room came from your place. Ones you hadn't finished. You can have them back if you want.'

Morgan ruffled the dark hair so like Becca's. 'You finished them, you get to keep them.'

'Cool.'

He vanished into the hall leaving Morgan alone with Becca. She busied herself unpacking the basket, clearly avoiding interacting with him.

'He's a clever lad, Becca.'

'Both of them are intelligent.' She leaned against the sink, her hands gripping the edge of the bench beside her hips. The jeans showed off her shape, showing the lean muscular thighs from cycling and the narrow waist. She had more curves these days, but motherhood would account for the increase in size of her breasts and hips. Her overall build was still slight, her bones fine.

'Is there anything I can do to help?'

'Can you chop vegetables?'

'If you supply me with a knife.'

They worked in silence for a time, her kneading dough for the pizza bases and him slicing and dicing the vegetables and tomatoes. 'Do you always make pizza from scratch?'

'Not always. It depends what I have in the pantry.'

This was what he'd dreamed of for years—family life lived simply. Time spent with a wife and children in the evenings. He might have had it all if he hadn't let jealousy overrule his good sense all those years ago. His best hope was as an outsider, watching his daughter and her mother living as a family with another man, with another child. He wouldn't marry now. Wouldn't have more children.

'Morgan? Is something wrong?'

He shook off the grief and forced a smile, putting the knife to use again. 'Sorry, I was off with the pixies.'

Her look was intent, searching his face as he focused on the job, not wanting her to see his vulnerability. If she had any idea of his feelings, she wouldn't allow these snatched moments. Wouldn't encourage or understand his need to pretend for a few hours he could have anything approaching a normal life.

***

It seemed strange having Morgan here. She'd resigned herself to never seeing him again, or only at a distance. Now she worked with him every day, and he was edging his way into her personal life. Because of the children. Or Gabby, anyway. He seemed to have made a connection with her. She couldn't help wondering why he hadn't brought a wife home with him. The way Grace talked, he'd had any number of women lined up for a happy ever after over the years. Yet here he was, still single. She patted out the dough onto the trays and slathered the tomato paste over the surface.

'I thought you might have been seeing Sabine tonight.'

Morgan looked up from grating the cheese. 'I'm meeting her tomorrow.'

He sounded so matter-of-fact, but her heart rebelled, squeezing tight in her chest. She'd been numb for so long, all her feelings tied up with the children, these aches and pains caused by Morgan's presence in her life were debilitating.

Forcing herself to remain calm, she started spreading the toppings. 'Seriously, Morgan. You don't have to spend time with Gabby and Edward. Don't let them nag you into doing things.'

He pushed away the board with the pile of cheese. 'I spend time with them because I choose to. You know why.'

Now she'd offended him. 'I won't stop you seeing them, but you'll be busy enough with work, without taking on the demands of two children who'll take up a lot of time if they have their way.'

'Why doesn't Dan help with the model building?'

'Dan? He wouldn't have the patience for a start. He's clumsy too. That's why Edward usually plays in their room.'

Morgan folded his arms, glowering across the table. 'Clumsy? Like you used to be clumsy?'

Darting a glance at the hall door, Becca shook her head. 'I've grown out of the awkward stage.'

'Were you ever clumsy? Or was there more going on?'

'It doesn't matter now. Things are different.'

'Is Dan abusive?'

Becca put the herbs in her hand down on the table. 'Why would you say that?'

'Because I've been thinking a lot about the past and I wondered if things were going on here I didn't know about. Things resulting in all those knocks and bruises.'

'It's in the past. Leave it, Morgan. It doesn't matter. Not anymore. Anyway, Dan isn't abusive now. He's gentle as a lamb. A bit prone to breaking things, but only as a result of the accident.'

She could see Morgan was about to say more, but Gabby wandered into the room, rubbing her eyes which lit up at the sight of Morgan sitting at the table.

'Hey, Morgan. I didn't know you were here.'

He draped one arm loosely over the girl's shoulders. 'I dropped in to see you but you didn't want to wake up.'

'You aren't going away now?'

'I'm staying for tea if you can spare me some pizza.'

'Mum always makes heaps. She likes cold pizza for breakfast.'

Becca's face heated. 'Only sometimes. When I'm running late for work.'

Morgan's eyes softened. 'Now I know your secret.'

Secrets. She'd had way too many of those, and now they were coming out. She'd never expected him to look back and see the past with clear eyes. Maybe it would make a difference in how he approached what happened with her. And Dan. Or maybe not. He was better off starting fresh with someone like Sabine, rather than trying to resuscitate what he'd had with the girl next door.

Grace might have softened for the sake of her grandchildren, but she wouldn't want Morgan to marry for the sake of those children. She'd made her position clear twelve years ago. Becca would never settle for that kind of marriage anyway. She'd dreamed of the kind of marriage where love held them together, not duty. Dreams she'd put aside under the weight of her own responsibilities.

It was a great evening. Surprisingly enough. Morgan had put aside any resentment he might have and entertained the twins with funny stories about his travels and children in the places he'd worked. They'd teamed up for scrabble, Morgan and Gabby against Edward and herself and it had been a close run, down to a couple of points, so Edward didn't feel shamed by being beaten by his sister. They'd insisted Morgan put them to bed, which was kind of sweet, considering they had long ago declared themselves too old to need tucking in.

Becca kept busy cleaning up the kitchen, keeping one ear open for the chatter and laughter coming from the bedroom. When they finally fell silent, she braced herself for Morgan's presence in the small kitchen.

He came in, his face sombre, and propped himself on the corner of the table. 'I enjoyed the time with the two of them.'

'It sounded like they enjoyed it too.'

'I wish ... It would have been nice to have the opportunity earlier.'

'You were away. You had your career.'

'If you'd told me I was a father, I would have made changes. I would have come home.'

'I know.'

'Then why didn't you tell me?'

'It wasn't a good time. You were still studying. You had plans. And ... well ... to be honest, I didn't think you'd believe me.'

'Would you ever have told me?'

She couldn't think of an answer to appease him which wouldn't be a lie. 'I don't know what might have happened.'

'You had Dan to consider too.'

'Yes. It was ... crazy.' It had been tough, those early years. A dying mother, Dan's condition. Aunt Bea's health failing. She'd had no choice but to agree with Grace's offer of help, and the conditions she set.

Morgan got to his feet, his expression drawn. It made him look his age in a way he hadn't while he'd been with the children. 'I know you have other commitments, but I want to spend as much time as I can with Gabby.'

'And Edward?'

'And Edward if he wants to join us. He's a nice kid and they're extremely close, aren't they?'

'Very close. You can't split them up.'

He scrubbed his long fingers through his hair. 'I'm learning that. You don't mind if Edward spends time with us?'

Becca stared at him, wondering why he was labouring the point. 'Why should I? I trust you to look after them properly.'

'What about Dan? Will it make problems there?'

'Dan finds them difficult. They can be pretty rambunctious. You'd be doing him a favour.'

'It's an attitude I can't understand. If I were...' He seemed to swallow his words. 'I appreciate you being so good about this.'

'As you said, you've missed out on years of growing up. I'm always aware of how much.'

His eyes darkened, the bright blue a pale ring around the pupil. 'I've missed a lot of things.'

He seemed too close suddenly, looming over her, his male scent spicy with a touch of basil from the pizza enveloping her. She swayed forward, inhaling his never forgotten essence. Clean soap and Morgan, his sensitive skin meaning he couldn't use fancy perfumed deodorants and aftershaves. There was an almost medicinal undertone this time, but not unpleasant.

His mouth was so close, all she had to do was stand on her tiptoes and she could taste him. What would he taste like now? Pizza, coffee? Something essentially him?

'I should go.'

In a daze, she watched him withdraw, picking up his car keys from the table. 'Okay. Goodbye then.'

He couldn't get away fast enough. Only pausing with the door half open. 'I'll contact you about seeing the children. I promised Edward I'd help him with *La Pinta*.'

'Sure. Um ... you could come to the birthday party next weekend if you're free? At the Hot Bread Place around three on Sunday.'

He nodded. 'Will do.'

The door shut behind him with a thud and his steps reverberated as he went down the broken stairs. She must get them fixed. At least they were fixable.

She pressed one hand against the tightness in her chest, feeling the slamming of her heart against her ribs. One thing that wasn't suitable for mending.

Her knees shook and it wasn't the reverberations from the wonky floor. Morgan was gone, heading out to his car. She flopped down on the nearest chair.

She'd almost kissed him. He had to have known.

Why else would he have run from the place as if pursued? By a needy woman who hadn't had sex in forever. No different from the needy girl she'd been at sixteen. Of course, he hadn't turned her down back then. He'd been nineteen and she'd known what boys were like. Morgan had admitted at the last he'd been no different to the rest. He'd been looking for an easy lay in the holidays and she hadn't been exactly shy about what she wanted. She'd wanted him. Any way she could get him.

It wasn't as if she was totally innocent at sixteen. She knew the facts of life. She'd been pushing Dan away for months, from the moment he'd realised Morgan was interested in her. He'd been wild when he figured out she'd given it up for Morgan Cavanaugh. If the accident hadn't happened, she'd known it was only a matter of time. With the drink and the drugs, he was out of control.

She expelled a shaky breath. The guilt was still there, after that first moment of relief when he'd come home from rehab and she'd known immediately the threat was gone.

After the twins were born, she'd had plenty of propositions from guys who thought she'd be an easy lay. Married guys, single guys. They didn't care, so long as they thought they could get some. She hadn't been tempted for a moment. The twins had to be her first priority; she didn't need to add to her already tarnished reputation.

She'd thought of leaving town once her mother passed away. Grace had offered to make her an allowance to help pay for the twin's care. Becca still didn't quite know why she hadn't taken the offer. It might have been possible before Aunt Bea came home with Dan. They could have all started somewhere else.

By the time she'd finished her training at the nursing home and the business degree at the clinic there was no time for second thoughts, the children were at school and she didn't want to uproot them. Once the promotion at the clinic came up, she hadn't considered moving again.

At least Morgan had a reason to keep her on at the surgery. If she lost her job, she'd have to leave town and he wouldn't want the twins to leave. Not when he was making a connection with Gabby. He'd made it clear enough. Today he seemed to have found something in common with Edward which gave him two reasons to stay. Two reasons to let her keep her job. Unless she blew it by letting him see she was attracted to him. Not hard at work, but if he was going to start coming by to visit the twins, she'd have to make sure not to give herself away.

Especially in public. There were a few people who might remember who she'd been hanging around with before the twins were born, without the dead giveaway of Gabby's resemblance to the Cavanaugh's absent son. Now he was home they could make the comparison without the misty glaze of fading memory. Today had already started them thinking. It would be up to Morgan and his parents as to how they met any gossip. Becca's lips had been sealed by her promise since the twins were born. So far she'd kept her side of the bargain and Grace had kept hers.

There had been no provision for what would happen if the tacit silence was broken. Not by either party, but by the knowing looks and curious tongues of the town. The twins had already guessed the truth, but they'd followed the adult's lead in keeping silent. If the other children started talking, it could hurt both of them.

A rattle at the door startled her, but it was Dan. Not that she'd expected Morgan to come back.

His clothes were filthy but he was beaming as he usually did coming back after a day on the farm. He'd miss it once he moved to Bialga, but maybe Thackery might know someone nearer there who could use an extra hand on weekends.

He placed a box of produce and a carton of eggs from the farm on the table and looked around the room with an expectant gleam in his eyes. 'Who's visiting?'

'No-one.'

'There's a four by four out the front.'

Morgan's car? 'We had Morgan Cavanaugh visiting earlier. Maybe he left his car there while he visited his parents.'

'Morgan Cav'nuh. I remember him.' His forehead wrinkled. 'I thought he was gone.'

'He's taking over Doctor Farrell's surgery.'

'Oh.' He seemed to lose interest, opening the fridge. He usually went to the hospital clinic in Bialga so he wouldn't be Morgan's patient anyway. 'Can I have some pizza?'

Becca sighed. 'Have one piece. Then you need to have a shower.'

'Okeydoke.'

He wandered off down the hallway munching his pizza. A few minutes later he was in the shower and by the time she'd finished her preparation for tomorrow's breakfast, he was in his room, leaving her free to go to bed.

One worry was gone. She'd half expected some animosity considering the ongoing friction between them when she'd been going out with Morgan. It might be a different matter from Morgan's point of view. He still had his memories and he'd had no time for Dan before he'd thought there was something between Becca and him.

And she'd gone and invited Morgan to the birthday party. She'd have to organise for them to meet beforehand in case something blew up.

She peered out the window at Morgan's car, still parked out the front, gleaming with frost in the moonlight. There was a light at the Maiden place. Morgan's place. He must have walked home. Had he been too angry to drive? Or too sickened by her almost-kiss? Nausea crawled along her gut. She didn't want to have to face him. Unfortunately, she'd have to. Every damn day if she was going to keep her job. She flicked off the light.

Tomorrow was another day. And she was going to have to face a man who had declared years ago in no uncertain terms that he didn't give a damn.

Chapter 7

Morgan shivered in the early morning chill. He'd been a fool to leave his car behind at Becca's place. He'd almost kissed her. She wasn't free but he'd wanted a taste. So. Damn. Much. His body was shaking so hard from the control he'd slammed on at the last minute, he'd needed to walk off the agitation. By the time he'd got back, the windscreens were solid with ice. It was simpler and quieter to go home and come back in the morning once the sun melted the frost.

He could see ice crystals glinting in the sunlight on the roof of the car, but it was already melting on the glass. A few minutes with the demister and he'd be good to go. Digging into his jacket pocket, he pulled out the keys. He hesitated, checking the windows of the house. Sunday morning they would be having a sleep in. Unless they were going to church.

'Hyah, Morgan.'

He blinked into the shadows on the far side of the house as a bulky figure in a maroon tracksuit and uggies emerged with a bottle of juice in one hand and a piece of toast in the other.

'Dan.' He was still easily recognisable with the extra weight, close cropped blond hair and two-day stubble with a touch of ginger. The ginger gave him pause, but he shook it off. There was no resemblance between him and either of the two children. Gabby's hair was pure red and Dan's eyes were a lighter shade of brown and different shape to Edward's and his skin tones tended to reddening under the sun before tanning.

The younger man leaned over the fence, dangling the toast and taking a swig from the juice. 'Nice car.'

Narrowing his eyes, Morgan studied the man's face. 'I bought it in Brisbane when I arrived back from Rwanda.'

'That's in Africa. I remember.' The words came out slow and a bit slurred. Was he drunk, or was this the result of the accident?

'I've been working there.'

Dan shifted awkwardly. 'I work at the Recycling Depot. In Bialga. With Gordon.'

Something cold iced its way down Morgan's spine. 'You like it there?'

'Yeah. The bus ride is boring. But soon I won't have to take the bus. I'm gonna live with Gordon and Bill and Tracey.'

'Are they your workmates?'

'Mostly. Tracey works at a café.' Morgan couldn't remember the sullen Dan ever grinning like this before. 'Tracey brings me cakes from the café sometimes.'

'Dan, what are you doing?' Becca's sharp tones brought both men around to look at her.

She was wearing an old-fashioned chenille dressing gown in a dark pink, her hair still mussed from bed. Morgan's heart lurched at how young she looked, barefoot and pink toed on the cold winter grass.

'I better go. See yah, Morgan.' Dan wandered off, taking bites out of his toast with mumbled murmurs of appreciation. Morgan suppressed a smile as the family dog dived out from under the house to scavenge a discarded crust and vanished again.

Becca stayed where she was, hands thrust into the pockets of the dressing gown. 'You didn't take your car.'

'I went for a walk and it was frosted by the time I came back.'

'I wondered if that was the difficulty. Although it shouldn't be with a fancy new car like yours.'

'You didn't marry Dan.'

Her brows rose over wide eyes. 'Marry Dan? Why would I...?' She glanced behind her but her step-cousin had already vanished into the house. 'I suppose this is about the children.'

'I always assumed they were his until I met Gabby and saw the family resemblance. And you changed your name.'

'I wasn't going to be called after Rodney Bujold. As soon as Mum passed away, I changed it back to Walters. It's always been my legal name, same as the kids. The creep never adopted me officially.' She huffed a breath that fogged the air. 'Dan's been like this since he got out of rehab. He has issues with concentration and memory. Among other things. Physical mostly. He can't cope with having the kids around much because the noise bothers him. Anyway, he has a girlfriend at Bialga.'

'Tracey?'

'How did you know?'

'She brings him cakes.'

A stain of colour marked her cheekbones and too late he remembered how often she'd brought him cakes she'd made when she was younger. To share with the other boys, but he'd always known they were for him.

'He's moving to Bialga shortly so I'm sure he'll enjoy being pampered by her.'

He wanted to ask about Edward, but she was already on the defensive. If she'd had a relationship after Gabby was born, it was none of his business. He wondered if she was in a relationship now. She wasn't married to Dan. So it wouldn't have been against his principles to kiss her. Although it wasn't an altogether sensible thing to do with things so fragile while he got to know Gabby.

He suppressed the excitement that brought his heart rate up. He wasn't any use to any woman. Not even Becca.

She shifted on the grass, curling her toes and a surge of guilt swept him for keeping her out in the cold. 'You better go back inside. I think the ice has pretty much cleared so I can head off.'

'It's all right. I'm used to the cold. The house is like a fridge anyway. But I'll let you go. You've got a date today.'

He wouldn't call it a date, but he should keep moving. 'Can I call by and see the kids this afternoon?'

'Sorry, we're going out. To visit some school friends.' She added the explanation quickly, as if she didn't want him asking where.

'I'll see you tomorrow at work, in that case.'

He climbed into the car, aware of her watching him. She was still standing there when he glanced in the rear vision mirror as he turned into his driveway.

*

He arrived home from his meeting with Sabine after three, satisfied with what had been organised. The early mark meant he had plenty of time before dinner, which made it a good time to go talk to his parents. He'd been putting it off because there'd never seemed to be the right moment. The evening meals were usually fairly rushed with him working full-time and he didn't linger afterwards, once he'd helped with the washing up. His father's health meant he needed plenty of rest and early nights were the norm.

His mother welcomed him with a wary gleam in her eye, as if she knew the reckoning was coming. There was no way she wouldn't have recognised the resemblance long ago. Not with the multitude of family photos on the walls and any spare surfaces. Four generations of Cavanaugh's and the Taite side from his mother. Gabby was a Cavanaugh through and through apart from the Taite nose.

'I'll make a cuppa.'

Morgan sat at the kitchen table, overwhelmed with a kind of nostalgia for the past. He'd spent a lot of time in this kitchen, usually with friends. As an only child, he'd found his playmates among the neighbours. His mother hadn't always approved of them, but she preferred them coming into her kitchen and eating her food, to running around town getting her golden boy into trouble.

She certainly hadn't approved of Becca's family. Once again, the priority had been keeping them under her nose and out of trouble. Only it hadn't quite worked the way she'd hoped.

Taking a sip of the freshly brewed tea, he waited for his mother to get comfortable before he spoke. 'I need to talk about Gabby Walters.'

'I thought you might.'

'Why didn't you tell me?'

Grace fiddled with her teaspoon. 'What would you have done if you'd known?'

'Asked Becca to marry me.'

'She was sixteen. Far too young to make a commitment like that. What on earth were you thinking, Morgan?'

'I was a nineteen-year-old male. What do you imagine I was thinking about?'

'There were always condoms in your bathroom. I expected you to use them. You were too young to take on so much responsibility.'

'And she wasn't? She was sixteen and pregnant. Way too much responsibility for a girl not out of school.'

'We helped. Your father and I. Right from the start.'

'But you couldn't tell me.'

'I know you, Morgan. You would have ruined your life, tying yourself down with a wife and family when you were starting out. Besides, you weren't well.'

Not well. A nice euphemism for a complete mental breakdown.

Grace never liked to refer to it. A combination of too much study, a crisis of faith over Brittany's death and Becca's betrayal.

He thought back to that time, struggling with his studies, medicated. Failing. He'd been so damned ashamed. It had only added to the spiral.

Those months all seemed rather vague from this distance. He'd blamed Becca. Would he have been as ill if he hadn't been so devastated by her betrayal? Perhaps the stress of learning he'd be a father at nineteen would have had the same effect. The chronic depression had dogged him for years as it was. Would parenthood have helped or hindered his recovery?

He'd never know for sure.

'How do you know Becca would have chosen to marry me? She's not married and she's close to thirty. Not exactly rushing into anything, is she?'

Grace snorted. 'Not marry you? What planet are you on? A girl like that. Of course she would have married you. It's probably why she got pregnant.'

'Seriously, Mum. You're blaming Becca for getting pregnant now? It was the usual thing. Contraceptive failure. I guess neither of us were experts on condoms because we certainly used them and she still got pregnant.'

Grace closed her eyes, brow creased. 'It's a long time ago. I don't remember exactly what I thought about the reasons behind her being pregnant. It was all about damage control.'

'I would have wanted to know. Becca should have told me. Not let me assume it was someone else's child.'

Meeting his eyes, his mother nodded wearily. 'She tried to. We ... I convinced her it wouldn't be wise.'

'You...' Hot rage balled in his throat. His mother had done this to him. The woman who was supposed to love him. To want the best for him. 'You stopped her?'

'Once we explained, she agreed it was the right thing to do. We promised to help out. Babysit mainly. She wouldn't take money. She's proud.' He recognised a note of surprise and a touch of respect in his mother's voice.

'Did you blackmail her into keeping silent?'

'Of course not. She understood our position. Because of her father.'

'What's her father got to do with it? He's been dead since before I left town.'

'Not Rodney Bujold. Her birth father, Doug Walters. He did the same thing and killed himself because of it.'

Morgan pushed the half empty cup away. 'I don't understand. What did he do?'

Grace pursed her lips. 'I thought Rebecca would have told you.'

'I know he died when she was small.' She hadn't talked much about her family at all. If she did it was usually her mother's illness. Even that was rare.

'Doug got Emmy pregnant at their school graduation party. He put off going to university and got a job so he could marry her but he wasn't cut out for working as a labourer and he couldn't keep a job. Then he was injured at the sawmill on his first day and they amputated a couple of fingers. It was disastrous. He was a promising musician. He lost his scholarship and eventually killed himself. Rebecca found him hanging in the old meat safe at the back of their place.'

He couldn't breathe. No wonder his mother had panicked. It must have seemed like history was about to repeat itself. Then the final words hit hard. 'Becca found him?'

'She probably doesn't remember. She must have been only three or four.'

'And then her mother married that pig. No wonder...'

He couldn't get the image of Becca as a child, hiding in the barn, out of his head. He had nothing to complain about. His childhood had been idyllic in comparison. He'd been so damned blind to what had been happening around him. Only as an adult was he beginning to see things clearly.

'Did you tell Becca about me?'

Grace wrinkled her nose. 'Of course not. Your private affairs are not for public consumption.'

'Surely she had a right to know why you didn't want me told?'

'She quite understood your studies were important.'

'And you were determined I wouldn't marry her. Even later, after I was finished studying and healthy again.'

'It was your choice to not come back. If you'd come back when you were asked, before you went overseas, we would have told you.'

The truth hit him square in the gut. He'd been avoiding coming home and his mother played on it for her own reasons. 'You didn't put up much of an argument.'

For the first time, she flushed, showing a mottled colour under her carefully powdered cheeks. 'That was a mistake.'

'It came down to keeping Becca and I apart, didn't it?'

Grace's brows drew together in memory. 'It seemed like the right thing to do. Your father didn't agree.'

'How did Becca feel about it?'

'I didn't ask. I suppose, looking back, she was disappointed. Before then she'd been quite receptive about going away and starting fresh. Once it was clear you weren't coming back, she settled in. Quite stubborn about it. I was surprised. I didn't think she had it in her.'

'Why not?'

'None of the Walters family came to much. No backbone. Doug was the best of them, and he threw it away.'

'How do you know all this?'

'I...' She glanced across at the kitchen door. 'I went out with Doug's uncle, Stephen Walters. Briefly. A sickly family. The boys all had asthma.'

His mother had dated someone in Becca's family? It didn't sound like her at all. 'Gabby hasn't inherited it, has she?'

'The girl is healthy as a horse. Edward had a touch of it when he was younger, but he seems to be growing out of it.'

He was getting as anxious as any parent over their children, including Edward. It was a disturbing feeling. Steering the conversation away from Becca and the children, he asked about his father's health.

'Better. He enjoys pottering around but he's not up to looking after the farm.'

'You've leased out most of the land?'

Ned answered from the door.

'Jordan was using it to run beef cattle. He hasn't done much since his accident, but he was saying he hoped to purchase a few head in the spring.'

Grace hurried to her feet. 'Look at the time. I'll have to put the kettle on again.'

She bustled about and the conversation turned to family connections and cattle. Morgan focused hard on listening, but his mind was elsewhere.

He should be angry with his mother but it was hard to blame her totally when he considered Becca's history. Both women would have been fearful of precipitating the kind of disaster they'd witnessed before. Especially with his own fragility at the time. He'd like to think he wouldn't have taken that way out. Becca couldn't have known about his illness. Grace wouldn't exactly want to spread that minor detail around about her perfect son.

His mother was right about their age. They'd both been too young for marriage. Who knows what would have happened if they had. Probably divorced after a couple of years and splitting their time with the children. So not much different, except Becca had borne the brunt of the burden and he hadn't got to know his daughter.

His father walked him out after the meal and stood at the fence. Morgan leaned beside him, looking across the paddocks to the road and the river lit by the full moon, and beyond, the lights of the town showing through the trees. In the stillness, he could hear the sound of cattle on the Durand place on the far side of his own acreage. His home. For the first time he was able to acknowledge how much he'd missed this place.

'Grace told me you'd asked her about Becca and the children this afternoon. About why we never told you.'

Morgan tensed, his hand gripping the post. 'I would have thought you'd have more sense, Dad.'

'I always thought you'd be home before long and it would all come out. The resemblance is so obvious. I never expected it to take twelve years for you to come home.'

Guilt stirred bile in his throat. He swallowed the bitterness. The regret. 'It should never have been kept a secret.'

'You'll get no argument from me. Grace and Becca had it all sorted out before I realised what was going on. I left them to it.'

Unspoken was the reproach at his distance. He could have come home any time over the last twelve years. It was his own fault. None of the conspirators would have expected it to last this long. His mother's aim had been merely to keep him from marrying before gaining his qualifications.

Becca's motivations were harder to establish. He needed to understand her point of view. He needed to understand exactly what was going on between her and Dan before the accident. He needed to know where she stood in terms of relationships. There was no way he was going to miss out on the rest of his daughter's life. She could be his only child if circumstances didn't change.

He was supposed to be good at diagnostics. It was a pity he hadn't applied himself to this problem years ago. At least now he could start working on a plan.

***

Karen wandered into the staff room and helped herself to coffee from the machine. She cast an eye over the grocery list Becca was working on. 'Can we have something apart from Digestives in the bickie barrel?'

'I think so. Morgan's approved a larger budget for incidentals.'

'He's in a good mood this week. Do you think he had a successful weekend?'

Becca frowned up at her colleague. 'What do you mean?'

Karen leaned on the bench and sipped at her coffee. 'Maybe he got laid.'

An image of him with the lovely Sabine seared the back of Becca's eyes. Maybe he had. She had no idea what the result of his lunch with the teacher might have been. Maybe they'd made a day of it. Maybe a night. He'd certainly been less sombre the last few days. More relaxed.

She forced her attention back to the job at hand. 'It's not our business.'

'If he marries a local, he's more likely to stick around.'

Becca wasn't sure which scenario was more painful. Either way the children were going to be hurt. Especially if Morgan started his own family and the twins were sidelined. It was the most likely scenario if he didn't leave town at the end of his three years. She wasn't sure if she should be relieved Karen obviously hadn't heard the gossip about Morgan and Gabby at the school working bee. For some reason it hadn't gone viral like she'd expected. Perhaps for some people it was old news and not worth discussing.

Karen suddenly straightened, a flush brightening her cheeks. 'Doctor Cavanaugh.'

'Morgan, please. I thought we'd established that much.' His eyes narrowed at the pair of them as if he'd overheard part of the conversation.

'I better get back to work.' Karen slid past him with a grimace at Becca to indicate she was thinking the same thing.

Becca glanced down at the notepad, keeping her pen hovering, hoping Morgan would take the hint and leave. He didn't, going over to the sink and running himself a glass of water.

'I need to talk to you.'

Trying not to reveal the anxiety his words triggered, Becca put down the pen. 'How can I help?'

'Birthday presents. For Gabby's party on the weekend.'

'You don't have to bring anything. I'm sure they'll be happy to see you. That's all that's required.'

'I've missed eleven birthdays. I'm pretty sure I owe a present or ten.' It came out with an edgy tension that told her his calm demeanour was camouflage.

'Gabby's getting a new bike. She's grown out of her old one. Edward is getting the *Endeavour* ship model he wants.'

He blinked before raising a brow. 'Edward is celebrating his birthday too?'

'Of course. His is Saturday and Gabby's is Sunday. We celebrate on the same day though. It's easier.'

'How in the world did you manage that?'

Becca grinned up at him. 'I didn't intend it.'

'I suppose I need to get him a present too. Should he get a bike as well?'

'Gabby's old bike will do the job. It's still in perfect condition.'

He leaned on the bench in the same place Karen had chosen minutes before. 'Are we not paying you enough?'

Avoiding his gaze, Becca stood up, needing to be at eye level. Or at least closer than sitting would get her. 'I'm extremely well paid. I have no complaints.'

'Why are you so short of money, in that case? Your house needs work, you don't have a car and you need to resort to free childcare from my parents.'

Her stomach turned over and she swallowed a ball of tension in her throat. 'I've been organising an alternative for their afternoon care. If it's a problem, I can make the change immediately.'

He shifted, suddenly near enough to rest one hand on her shoulder. 'Don't take me the wrong way. I've no objection to the children spending time with my parents. It's logical and convenient considering how close you live. I simply want to know if you need financial help. I should be taking some responsibility. Do you need help?'

His grip on her shoulder burned right through the thin cotton of her shirt. 'We manage.' At his raised brows, she shifted uneasily. 'I have a mortgage to pay off. It makes things tight. But I'm getting there. I'm almost ready to buy a car.' She wasn't going to tell him his arrival had forced her to reconsider the expenditure. 'I don't like going into debt.'

'Fair enough. Why don't you sell the place? With the location on the river you should get a good price, even if the house is worthless. You could pay out the mortgage and look at something better in town.'

Something his mother had urged for years. Preferably as far away from the Cavanaugh home as possible. Maybe she could consider it once

Dan was settled. He wouldn't have coped with a move back then. It had taken a lot of preparation with his support team to get him to this point. 'It wasn't convenient at the time.'

'You were considering it?'

'Maybe. Your mother suggested I might like to try Bialga. It would be a bigger school for the children and more opportunities.'

His hand dropped. 'My mother suggested it? I don't see why she would.' He compressed his lips and closed his eyes briefly. 'You're thinking of moving away?'

Maybe she should. If he was going to keep disrupting her life. Drive her insane with wondering about who he might be dating. Who he might marry. She forced a dismissive shrug. 'I'm not making a decision today.'

'I thought you liked your work.' He seemed almost lost, his words coming out in a whisper.

'It's a good job, but I have to think about what's best for the children.'

His expression hardened. 'The moment I discover I'm a father, you're planning to move away. You're aiming to cut me out of your life?'

Regret at her careless words tightened her gut. 'No. No. I wouldn't do it. Not now. They'd never forgive me.'

He slumped back on the bench, his eyes closed, head tilted to gaze blindly at the ceiling.

There was a faint beading of perspiration on his forehead. This mattered to him. It hadn't occurred to her he was already so attached to the children. They loved him, but he was so cool and contained, she hadn't considered it might be mutual. Something more than duty.

Chapter 8

Morgan couldn't totally contain his excitement at attending the children's birthday party. His first. He'd finally found something for them, with help from his parents. He'd decided to get the same thing for both children, so hopefully there would be no angst about favouring Gabby over the boy.

He was finding more and more in common with Edward as he spent time with both children. So much so he was starting to weave impossible dreams. Impossible because while he could be a father, at present, there was no possibility of him being a husband. The frustration of his slow recovery had been tempered until he'd found out Becca was unattached. Now he was anxious to see if his return to full health would return other functions. If not, he'd have little to offer the mother of his child.

He loved what they'd done with the walkway along the creek, the different shops opening out onto timber decking. The entrance off the main street was marked with a beautifully painted sign designating it The Creek Walk, with a picture of a pelican perched on the extended stroke of the K in creek. The pelicans weren't anywhere to be seen as Morgan approached the group hovering outside the Hot Bread Shop with its folk art rendered sign.

The two children spotted him first and came to meet him with welcoming grins, Gabby taking his free hand as if she'd been doing it all her life. Edward darted him a shy smile and walked beside him, occasionally glancing at the gift bags with curious eyes.

Without conscious thought, Morgan sought out Becca, finding her talking seriously with Thackery Harmsworth. She was wearing a pretty yellow blouse and light brown woollen trousers with a darker brown cardigan. Not fashionable but practical in this climate.

Thackery was dressed slightly less outrageously today in jeans, sheepskin boots and a jacket covered in sewn on patches. His hair was roughly fixed in a bun and his vivid eyes looked down at Becca with a tenderness that caught at something in Morgan's chest.

Beside him was Dan, neatly dressed in eighty's style brown corduroy trousers and jacket over a fair isle knitted sweater. Morgan would have bet money Thackery had done Dan's shopping at the local thrift shop. The result, he had to admit to himself, was good and Dan was happy enough watching the ducks on the creek.

Thackery saw Morgan first and nodded, bringing Becca's attention around. Her smile widened and then quivered as her gaze drifted over the three of them. It paused at Gabby's hand in his and he wondered what she was thinking behind those obscuring glasses. Was she pleased at the obvious rapport he was developing with Gabby, and with Edward, or did it threaten her somehow?

'Hi, Morgan. Good of you to come.'

'I'm pleased to be here.' He could see his parents inside the shop now, seated at a large table by the window.

Becca gathered up the group and shepherded them into the shop and seated them around the table, placing Morgan between the two children. Morgan recognised Marcia Kavocik beside the counter talking to a talk, dark haired man in jeans and a leather jacket. He seemed vaguely familiar.

'It's Tony Field. OMG. He is the best,' Gabby hissed.

The whole group turned to look.

Edward wrinkled up his nose. 'Don't be stupid. Why would he be here?'

Grace answered in her measured tones, picking up the menu card. 'He came for the wedding. You would have seen him there.'

Becca finished settling Dan and turned to Morgan. 'Ashleigh got married.'

Ashleigh. She was one more person he'd lost touch with over the years of his self-imposed exile. Not that they'd been close. He'd had no close friends here. Not the kind who would invite him to weddings. When he'd left, only Becca had tempted him to look back. He'd fought it, and the results had been disastrous.

'It was a lovely wedding. Tony Field was the best man, all dressed up in a gorgeous suit.' Gabby said it with a dreamy look in her eyes. Morgan had a horrible thought his daughter might have been imagining herself in the role of bride. Maybe with Tony Field. Luckily, Tony looked pretty well occupied.

Becca gave their order to the girl at the counter and returned to the table, checking Dan was okay on the way back. He was trying to think of something to say to her to open an innocuous conversation when they were interrupted.

'Morgan Cavanaugh?'

He returned Tony's smile and shook hands automatically. Marcia hovered, winking at the children as she slid a plate of beautifully decorated cupcakes and their drinks onto the table. Gabby was so enthralled at the sight of her hero close up she didn't glance at the cakes. The rest of the group murmured greetings,

Edward's being muffled by a mouthful of bright orange cupcake.

Morgan pulled himself together. 'Hi, Tony. I hear you're doing great things on the acting front.'

The soapie star smiled, one corner tucked in. 'I've been doing okay. I see you haven't hung about with settling down. Two kids already?'

An uneasy silence invaded the group and Tony jumped as if bitten and shot a confused glance at Marcia who was smiling too wide, her hand suspiciously close to Tony's wrist. She'd turned out gorgeous. Morgan couldn't blame Tony for looking at her like she was the best kind of cake.

Becca was looking green and wide eyed, a flush building on her cheeks. Morgan wasn't game to look at his mother. He kept his smile fixed. 'Sorry, Tony, no such luck. We're here to celebrate a couple of birthdays. I've recently returned from several years in Africa.'

Fortunately for everyone, Gabby jumped in, digging out a bright pink notepad and pen from her mini backpack. 'Can I have your autograph, Mr Field?'

'Sure you can, honey.' With good humour he crouched down beside the excited girl and scrawled something on the blank page. 'Here you go.'

'Can I have a kiss? That would be so awesome.'

With a laugh and a quick glance at Marcia, Tony complied with a peck on her cheek before retreating to the back of the store.

'I can hardly wait to tell my friends at school.' She sighed and touched her cheek. 'He is soooo gorgeous.'

Edward screwed up his face. 'You are so creepy. Why would you want a kiss from an old guy?'

'I'm never washing my face again. Besides, you'd be the same if it were Jimmy Maddox.'

'I love his music. I wouldn't want him to kiss me. Blech. Besides, I've already met him, last time he was here for a concert. He autographed my cd case from his first album.'

Becca brought the argument to a close by handing around the drinks. Before long they were happily eating and drinking, the contest over their favourite stars forgotten.

Becca still looked rather sick. His mother was carefully avoiding the subject, talking to Thackery about the organic vegetables he supplied. It was an odd group and he leaned back so he could talk past Gabby, who leaned on the table, treating a large pink-iced cake like an ice-cream.

'Were any of their friends invited?'

Becca straightened, taking a deep breath. 'We had a few school friends over yesterday for lunch. While Dan was at the farm. Today is strictly family.'

He nodded in understanding. 'I have presents. Should they open them here or take them home? The protocols of birthday parties are new to me.'

'Open them here. You'll like to see their reaction.'

'I would. At least I think I will. It's odd buying something for children you don't know well. I got something useful, I hope.'

The colour was returning to her face. 'They'll love anything you get them.'

The wry tone told him she was ambivalent about her children's acceptance of him in their lives.

He lowered his voice. 'I'm sorry if you were embarrassed by Tony's assumption.'

'Oh no. It was logical I suppose, seeing us together. He couldn't have known.'

'Surely he would have heard.'

'He was another one who left and never came back. Until now.' She paused, frowning across the store at where the actor had been. He'd gone at some point, without Morgan noticing. With a faint smile she shook her head.

'We should think about finishing up. Did you want to give them their presents first?'

Gabby shifted back in her seat. 'We aren't fussy, Morgan. Presents are always awesome. I got a bike from Mum and clothes from Grace and Grandpa Ned.'

'I got my *Endeavour* project,' Edward added, wiping icing from his cheek and licking it with relish. 'And clothes.'

Becca raised her eyebrows ruefully at Morgan. 'Clothes are always useful.' Her expression said she appreciated them more than the children.

Edward perked up. 'Thackery gave us a wind-up torch each. It never runs out of battery. What are you giving us?'

Taking the hint, Morgan handed over the gift bags. He hoped he'd got it right. He'd checked with his mother, who seemed to think the gifts were extravagant but appropriate. Useful.

Gabby was the first to unwrap her parcel, tearing off the store gift wrapping with total disregard for the paper. 'Wow. This is the awesomest.'

She held up the computer tablet for everyone to see. 'Thanks, Morgan. It's perfect.'

He couldn't see Becca's reaction with Gabby jumping all over the place. Edward had opened his identical tablet and smoothed his hands over the case with quiet pride. 'It's really good. Now we won't have to share.'

Gabby left her seat to move around the table to show Grace and Ned.

Finally, he could see Becca, unobtrusively dabbing at her face. She caught his gaze on her and smiled. 'It's wonderful. I should say it's too much, but they do need them for school.'

Edward carefully slid his gift back into the bag. 'Thanks, Morgan.'

'Couldn't have you fighting with your big sister when you have assignments.'

'Nah. We don't fight much. Anyway, she's only bigger because she's tall. I'm still the oldest.'

The room tilted as Morgan tried to focus on Edward. 'The oldest? But ... how?'

'I was born at seven minutes to midnight and Gabby was born at eighteen minutes past. That's how come we have different birthdays.'

'Twins?' He snapped his mouth shut over a curse, conscious of Edward staring at him. His heart pounded hard in his chest, raising a sweat that trickled down his spine.

Twins. Both children were his.

'Didn't you know?' He leaned forward. 'Mum. Morgan didn't know we were twins.'

The attention of the whole table was on him as Morgan turned to Becca.

Her pallor had an undertone of green again. 'How could you not know? Everyone knows.'

'It was never mentioned. I mean, they don't look alike. I never guessed.'

Gabby leaned on Ned's shoulder. 'So you thought it was only me?'

Catching sight of Edward's worried frown, Morgan shrugged. 'I knew you were a package deal. A two for one.' He put his arm around Edward's thin shoulders. 'We're getting to be good mates, aren't we? That's what's important.'

The boy relaxed into his hold and Morgan let out a breath. A son. And a daughter. He let himself glance over at his mother. She was almost as pale as Becca. He'd let her get away with it when he'd thought Becca had moved on and had another child with someone else. But this was too much.

He shifted in his seat. If he didn't get away, something was going to break, and there was no way it was going to be him. Not in public like this.

'I have to go do something at the surgery. Check some test results. Please excuse me.'

Both children murmured their dismay, but he had to move.

He stood, circling to grip the back of the seat. 'It's been great. I'll catch you later, kids.'

He flicked a glance at Becca. 'If it's all right with you, I'd like to come over this evening.'

'Sure.' She half rose and then plopped down. 'Any time.'

***

Becca watched Morgan walk away. He was going in the wrong direction for the surgery, but perhaps he was getting his car from the large public carpark on the other side of the shopping centre. Only Dan seemed unperturbed by the little scene, being given a serviette by Thackery who had offered to come along and help keep Dan occupied. At least Becca could be sure Thackery would keep his mouth shut about the events of the day. He would probably tell Win, but his sister was even more discreet than Thackery.

Morgan hadn't known. She stared at Grace, who had assured her Morgan knew everything and was quite all right with it. Becca was pretty sure neither of those statements were correct.

He hadn't realised Edward was his child. It explained a lot. It certainly explained why she'd sensed a reluctance in Morgan to engage with Edward.

He must have thought Dan had fathered him, if his belief she'd married Dan had any truth.

He'd known for a week Dan wasn't involved, so who did he think was Edward's father?

Shaking her head, she started gathering up the gifts and stacking the empty plates. 'Time to go.'

At least the twins seemed to have weathered the storm. Edward clung to Morgan's gift like it was a lifeline. Extravagant, but as Morgan had pointed out, he had a lot of birthdays to catch up on. As they scrambled into Ned's car, Grace at the wheel, she frowned. He'd given Edward an equally valuable gift, though he claimed not to know the boy was his son at the time. Which had to mean something.

At home, they vanished into their room with the presents and she was able to relax with a cup of tea while she waited for Thackery and Dan to arrive. It wasn't long, Thackery pulling into the driveway with the funny old truck he used for his deliveries only ten minutes later. She went out to thank him for his help.

Dan scrambled out and wandered inside. To her surprise, Thackery also jumped down from the cab and shut the door. 'Morgan followed us out of town so he'll be home any moment. Do you want me to keep an eye on Dan and you can go and see him?'

Even as he spoke, Morgan's car turned into his driveway across the road. Thackery was probably right. It would be best to go and speak to him alone, without the hindrance of little ears.

'Thanks. I'll do that.'

She followed him inside and he settled down with Dan in the lounge room with the television and a stack of action movies. They wouldn't watch more than one in the time she'd be away, but Dan liked to choose from a selection of his favourites.

Freshening up in the tiny, old-fashioned bathroom, Becca debated putting on make-up. She rarely used it and she put down the lipstick, picking up the clear gloss she used to moisturise her lips.

There was no point trying to impress Morgan. Trying to vamp him. She smoothed her palms down the tan slacks she'd worn for the party and re-tucked the pale lemon blouse, twitching the cardigan sleeves down over her wrists.

Neat and clean. It was the lowest common denominator to dress for, but she was a single mother of twins. She had better things to worry about.

She decided to walk, hoping the fresh evening air and exercise might soothe the achy gallop of her heart.

He wouldn't stand for half-truths and evasions. It had to be the whole truth and nothing but the truth. She owed him that, now Grace had withdrawn her ultimatum.

It would have been easier years ago, before the children were old enough to understand. She and Morgan were going to have to stop frittering about on the edge of things and make some solid plans on how to co-parent. Which involved sitting down and talking to the twins about how the future was going to look.

The house was in darkness, but Morgan's car was in one of the sheds, the timber doors left ajar.

'Morgan?'

The door gave way under her hand, opening into the back porch with its usual clutter of boots and a couple of jackets hanging from hooks. She slipped off her dusty shoes and placed them alongside the boots.

The kitchen was empty and she ventured into the shadowy hallway. 'Morgan? Are you home?'

She passed a bathroom and several empty bedrooms and finally an enormous lounge room overlooking the front stairs. All empty. She suppressed the urge to assuage her curiosity about the house. Maybe he'd walked across to his parents' place for dinner.

Backtracking, she went down a side hallway that led to a sunroom and some more bedrooms.

It had been years since she'd been a visitor in this lovely old Queenslander. She'd expected him to be in the master bedroom at the front of the house, near the lounge room, but perhaps he was using one of the other rooms opening onto the side verandah.

'Morgan?'

A whisper of sound drew her to one of the bedrooms. The bed was empty and she almost turned away when the faint silhouette against the window impinged on her consciousness.

'What do you want?' His voice came thick and hoarse, as if he were fighting a cold.

Becca hesitated, one hand steadying herself on the doorframe. 'I thought we needed to talk.'

A rumble of rusty laughter shivered the cool air in the room. 'Slightly overdue, isn't it?'

'Your mother didn't tell you about Edward? That they were twins?'

'No. She danced around the topic as if the truth were too nasty a proposition to face.'

'You're angry with us.'

He turned around, his face a blur in the dimness. She reached for the light switch.

'No. Leave it off.'

Her hand dropped to her side. 'We did you a terrible wrong. I don't know how to ask you for forgiveness. I probably shouldn't try. I am sorry. For what it's worth.'

'I thought ... I thought I could forgive you if you'd moved on. If there'd been someone else in your life. If you'd built a family and your silence was to protect your family. But that didn't happen. I can't see any other reason for keeping it from me. Not for twelve years.' He moved closer, away from the window, vanishing into the shadows in the centre of the room. 'Tell me I'm wrong. Tell me you had built yourself a family to protect. If there was someone, where did they go?'

'There was no-one. No excuse. No-one, nothing to protect but ourselves.'

'Protecting them from what? Who? From me?'

'At first, it was about protecting you. Your future. Grace made me promise. At the time it seemed fair enough. Afterwards, when you didn't come back, it was about keeping the status quo.'

'The status quo. How many people knew? How many people are out there thinking I'm some kind of louse for abandoning my pregnant girlfriend and my children?'

Becca squinted to try and see him through the gloom. The light from the window had faded entirely. Only the paleness of his face stood out, not clear enough to see any expression. 'Hardly anyone knows. Not for sure. You'd already been gone from town for years, at boarding school and uni, so most people didn't make the connection. We never went on proper dates or anything.'

The faint rustle of movement halted. 'Didn't we? No. You're right. We never did go out together. Did you mind?'

Automatically she went to say no, but her determination to speak the truth halted her. The darkness made it easier. 'Yes. I think I did at the time. I was like any girl who wanted to show off her boyfriend.'

'You didn't get much that was worthwhile from me in the end.'

'I got our children. They're worth everything.'

'Is that why you kept them secret? Some kind of revenge?'

'It wasn't about revenge. I didn't think you'd believe me.'

He was moving again. A sharp click and a pool of light blossomed beside the bed. It left his face in shadow, illuminating the bedside table, the patchwork quilt of the double bed and the black shirt and trousers he'd worn to the party. The grey knit jumper he'd worn under the jacket lay on the bed, as if he'd tossed it there when he arrived home.

'Because of the argument about your relationship with Dan?'

Becca nodded, skirting him to perch at the end of the bed. 'I wasn't sure about being pregnant that night. I had the symptoms but I wasn't game to get a test kit locally. I was going to tell you and ask if you could get a test kit in Brisbane.'

He dropped onto the side of the bed, an arm's length away, loosely clasping his hands and resting them on his knees. The shade of the lamp still left his face in shadow. 'And I broke up with you.'

'It would have happened sooner or later.'

A hiss told her he'd sucked in a breath, but his voice remained flat and cool. 'Why do you say that?'

'People like me...' She broke off with a shake of her head. 'You were in Brisbane most of the time. I couldn't expect you not to notice a whole city full of attractive women.'

He snorted, something almost like a laugh. 'A whole city. You do have an exaggerated idea of my stamina.'

'You know what I mean.'

'When I was in Brisbane I was head down, tail up studying like a lunatic. I didn't have time to breathe, never mind spend my time partying. I was doing a double degree in biological sciences in order to get a head start with the tropical medicine component later on. It's why...' His words trailed off and she had a feeling he'd been about to say something important.

'Anyway, we broke up and you thought I'd been seeing Dan on the sly. How could I tell you I might be pregnant?'

'What was the truth about Dan? You might as well tell me. It's not going to change anything now.'

'I didn't want him and he didn't want me. Not really. He wanted to get the upper hand on the stuck-up Morgan Cavanaugh. He hated that you dumped him as a friend and he knew you'd tried to get Ben to steer clear.'

'Did he force you into anything? Did he hurt you?'

'He slapped me around a couple of times. Nothing I couldn't handle.'

Except the last time. That had scared her. If Morgan hadn't dropped by early...

'He was out of it with drugs and alcohol most of the time. He dropped out of school ages before. The police had been onto him and it made him angry.'

'So he took it out on you.'

'He wasn't home much. The only time he came home was to get money out of Aunt Bea.'

'Was he getting money that last night? The night of the accident?'

'He'd been into the tea caddy. Mum used to hide a bit of cash there for emergencies. He found it and I tried to stop him.'

'He wanted it for drugs?'

'I'm guessing it was. He had some with him in the car that night.'

'I remember.'

***

Morgan watched Becca flex her toes in the black socks she was wearing. She was studying them as if they held the answer to the secrets of the universe.

The anger still burned inside, pushing at his vitals, churning his stomach and tightening his chest. So much anger. At Becca, at his parents. At Dan who'd hurt Becca and lied about her. Dan was beyond punishment now, his life strangely happier with all that resentment and bitterness burned out of him by the accident. The guilt still tied his gut all the same.

'I wanted Dan to be dead that night. I thought if he died, I could go back.'

Becca's head jerked around to face him. 'Is that why you didn't want me to help with CPR?'

'It was more I hated you touching him.'

'I hated it too. I could taste him. It was foul.' She brushed her fingers over her knees. 'I felt guilty about him. Not then. Later. When he came home from rehab with Aunt Bea and I realised he was different. I was relieved and it made me feel awful. He was nice and I should have been sorry about the accident but I couldn't help being happy he was changed. I had the twins to worry about by then. I couldn't have risked them if he was like he was before the accident.'

'I wondered if I could have done more. For him and for Brittany. I was planning on being a doctor. I should have been able to do something.'

'But you weren't a doctor. You hadn't done more than your first aid training, same as me, plus eighteen months of your science degree.'

'That's what ... what everyone told me. It still bothered me.'

She was so close. He wanted to reach out and touch her. Needed to comfort her. To be comforted. He'd lost the right when he'd rejected her all those years ago. He'd lost it when he'd been too cowardly to come home and face her. Too ashamed.

'Tell me about the twins. They were early, weren't they?' He'd known the date and at the time it had proved to him Becca's baby couldn't be his. If he'd known she had twins would he have figured it out? It was stupid trying to second guess the past. His head had been in a different space back then. Trying to justify his actions. His failures.

'Almost six weeks early. They came fast. They tell you the first birth takes ages. Not with my two. Doctor Farrell said they must have had roller skates.'

Doctor Farrell. Those cryptic remarks made sense now. 'Was it a hard labour?'

'I remember I was terrified. Not the pain so much. Edward was a bit sluggish which worried them and they flew him to Brisbane to the ICU. Gabby was better but they decided to send her down too.'

'You should have let me know then. I could have come visit.'

'Your mother said you still had exams.' She tilted her face up, her eyes scrutinising him. Accusing him. 'Would you have come?'

Would he have come? Maybe to get a glimpse of Becca. But to see the twins? 'I don't know. I was pretty mixed up.'

They'd said it was exam fatigue and his parents had forcibly taken him away on holidays. A complete break. *Breakdown?* Maybe it was after then when his mother had made her agreement with Becca. She'd been horrified at his mental state. Ashamed too. As if his weakness somehow tarnished her.

Becca picked up his sweater and folded it. It was a strangely maternal thing to do and the grip on his heart tightened painfully. Her small hand with its competent fingers and short practical nails smoothed over the wool of the jumper. He caught a drift of her scent. It reminded him of his mother's garden.

Sweet peas and pinks. His mother called them dianthus, but Morgan liked the cottagey sound of pinks. Sweet with a touch of cloves. Still the same as years ago.

She'd been grubby a lot as a kid, much to his mother's disgust, but once she was in her teens she became fanatical about cleanliness. Her clothes may have been shabby, but they were always clean and she smelled sweet. He sucked in another taste of her, hoping for more of a reaction. Nothing. But he liked it anyway. It brought back good memories.

Her voice was almost tentative. 'I have heaps of photos of the twins on my computer. From when they were babies. I could give you copies.'

'I'd like to have them.' *Love to have them.*

There didn't seem to be anything else to say. Even though he knew they needed to talk about the future. Maybe it would be easier now they'd touched on the past.

'Morgan? Was there anyone special for you? While you were away.'

Anyone special? He tried to think back over the years. They'd been empty years on the personal front. Full and sometimes satisfying on the professional side of things. Sometimes terrifying. Sometimes dreadful. Too much death. He wouldn't be going back. He'd been kidding himself to think he could spend three years recuperating and then fling himself back into it. It was emotionally draining. Physically exhausting. He also had children to consider now.

'No. No-one special.' It would be pointless to lie. Only the truth would serve to build the kind of understanding they'd need to co-parent the twins. Most of the truth. Some things he couldn't share. The pain bit into his chest and he sucked in a calming breath.

'Me neither.' She shifted on the bed, somehow coming closer. 'I did date a few people. You know what it's like, people trying to set up the single parents. I pretty much know who all the single dads are in town.'

Morgan didn't like that. Then it hit him. 'I'm a single dad now. I guess. Does that mean the matchmakers will be out in force?' He was still getting used to it. Father to twins.

'Maybe.' A wry smile curled her mouth. 'Unless you find yourself someone quick smart.'

A faint recollection nudged at him. 'What did you mean when you said "people like you"?'

A flush darkened her cheekbones. 'What you said when we broke up. That people like me shouldn't expect too much. That we were bound to be disappointed. It's true. You only have to look at my family.'

'I didn't mean it.'

He'd said it. It was funny. Not in the laughing sense. Many things over the last twelve years were hazy, but some things from before stood out with an almost cinematic clarity. The night of the accident, the scene of carnage he and Becca had come across an hour after the confrontation with Dan. The oh so cool and rational Morgan Cavanaugh had been a mess, hardly sane afterwards. Yet every word, every action was blazoned on his memory.

He'd been angry then, believing Dan's assertions that hot little Becca had turned to him for sex while Morgan had been away at university. Unconsciously he'd borrowed his mother's language to put Becca in her place.

Cut her as he'd been cut. *People like her.* In his mother's eyes, nothing could be more damning.

He'd known Becca was keeping things from him and the long months away had made him realise how much she meant to him. How much he relied on her. Maybe his guilt over his inability to help Dan had given the accusations more credit than they deserved. They'd already argued before they hopped in the car. After coming across the accident and trying to help, he'd been crazy mixed up, so hyper he'd attacked her verbally the moment they'd been left alone. Before he realised what was happening, he'd broken it off with Becca. He hadn't allowed himself to regret it. But together with everything else, that pretence had sent him spiralling into a very dark place.

'I didn't mean it, Becca. It was the worst thing I could think of to say.'

'You don't think accusing me of cheating was worse?'

'I...'

Morgan stared at her face, softly lit by the lamp. It reminded him of the other time that sat clearly in his memory. The other moment that had an almost luminescent quality to it. Becca in his room, seducing him with her soft hands and sweet mouth. With the love she'd offered freely. He'd tried hard to be good. To be responsible. So there was guilt there as well, and a kind of resentment when she could tempt him beyond his endurance. She'd been his first too. He'd played around a bit when he'd first gone to Brisbane. Before Becca.

Somehow, he'd never gone all the way. He'd been painfully shy around girls. It made him hold back. He wanted it, like most teenage boys, but never enough to be out of control. Enough to know what she was offering, in her bright innocence, was going to be amazing.

He forced out the response. 'I didn't think of it that way. I didn't know you could be hurt by the truth.'

'It wasn't true.'

'No. My stupid mistake.' More guilt. More regret.

Was he never going to get beyond his mistakes? Ever deserve the gift unexpectedly dropped in his lap?

Two beautiful children. Amazing children. With a wonderful mother he'd never in his wildest dreams come to deserve.

She was strong. Much stronger than he could ever be. He'd fallen at the first hurdle. Fallen so far it had taken years to pick himself up, even with the help of his doctors. It had been a miracle he'd made it through medical school. It had needed all his focus. All his attention. His mother had been right. He couldn't have coped with more.

Some of the anger drained away, lanced by the realities of the past. There was still his own culpability. No wonder she thought he was only using her. Quite apart from the fact that he'd told her that's what he was doing when they broke up.

An easy lay. His father wasn't a man to use violence on his son, but he'd always been strict about disrespecting women. If he'd known about Morgan saying something derogatory to Becca he'd have given him a clip under the ear and enough work on the farm to keep his mouth shut for months.

'We never went on a date?'

'Never.'

'Kind of backwards. Should we go on a date now?'

Becca twisted to face him, one knee brushing against his thigh. 'A date date? You're joking, aren't you?'

Her tone pretty much squashed any hopes she thought of him as a suitable partner for a romantic outing. He hadn't been thinking.

'We need to get to know each other better. Talk about how we should handle things. We could do it over dinner.'

'You aren't thinking of anything permanent?'

Her tone was so flat, she could have walked on it. Permanent sounded good. But impossible.

'I want to make this workable for the sake of the children. I can't offer anything else.'

'What *can* you offer?'

She was leaning close enough for him to feel her warmth. Her eyes glinted with a need that set him aching. Her tongue darted out to swipe along her lush bottom lip. The tension in his body, in his gut was almost painful.

When her mouth touched his, it was the brush of fairy wings, sweet and soft. There was no pressure, only a trickle of sensation along the sensitive flesh. Her hand cupped his jaw, holding him in place. She didn't need to. He couldn't have moved if he wanted to.

Twelve years and more vanished in a wisp of warmth taking him back to somewhere that remained a dream. He closed his eyes, letting feeling do the work. Listening to soft breaths and sensing a body which couldn't, wouldn't respond. Moisture pricked at his lids as she released him, a last stroke of her lips lingering at the corner of his mouth.

Blinking against the light, he caught a sparkle on her lashes and he swallowed the emotion. 'I can't offer you what you want. It has to be about the children.'

'Only the children?'

He nodded, the pressure in his throat too tight to allow speech.

She stood, discarding the jumper onto the bed, refolding it with trembling fingers. 'Very well. No dates. Only meetings about the children. Do you want to do this legally?'

The sudden harshness of her voice struck him in the chest. 'Legally? Yes. That would be best.' He could make sure they were all taken care of through a lawyer. Becca shouldn't have to struggle to pay bills. This way, pride couldn't get in the way. 'Who do you suggest?'

'Toby Mallings. Sabine's brother. He's been your parents' lawyer since his father retired.'

'I remember him. I'll contact his office tomorrow.'

He wanted to keep her here, but he couldn't make promises he might not be able to keep.

She was already halfway out the door.

Chapter 9

'Stupid. Stupid. Stupid.' Becca hopped down the back steps, trying to pull on a recalcitrant shoe.

Why had she thought he'd respond to her kiss? He was like a stuffed dummy. Not like before. He couldn't resist her when they'd been teenagers.

She'd been in love. Thought she'd been in love. At sixteen it was probably infatuation. And hormones. Definitely hormones on his side. She'd been stupid back then too. Thinking the friendship they'd shared for years meant she was more than a convenient lay when it turned physical.

It was hard trying to sort out the truth of what happened nearly thirteen years ago. It was nearly half her life away. She'd been only a few years older than the twins.

She halted at Morgan's gateway. So damn young. At least they weren't like her. Needy. Desperate to be loved. Or were they? They'd taken to Morgan easily, as if they had a dad-shaped hole in their hearts perfect for slotting him into their lives. Was that any protection?

The lights were on at home and it was past dinner time. She'd wasted ages with Morgan and they were still no further forward. Unless you count his wanting to see a solicitor. She picked up the pace, jogging past Thackery's truck and up the back stairs.

Thackery was at the sink, washing up.

'Where are Gabby and Edward?'

'In bed. Gabby pretty much flaked out after tea. I gave them veggie pasta.' He slotted another plate into the rack. 'Dan is watching a movie.'

Becca slumped onto a chair. 'Thanks. I lost track of the time.'

'No worries. How did it go with Morgan?'

Thackery was non-judgemental making it easy to respond. She knew it wouldn't go further. 'We cleared up a few things. Morgan is going to make an appointment with the solicitor to do things properly.'

'Is he planning to pay child support?'

Becca frowned. 'I don't know. We didn't discuss it.'

Thackery stared at her, a tea towel bunched in his hand. 'Did you talk about how things are going to work with the twins? Shared custody, visiting rights. Those minor details?'

Shared custody. She hadn't considered it. Her heart hammered in her chest as she gazed up at Thackery. 'Will I have to let him take them for weekends and holidays?'

'I imagine so. They're his children and he has parental rights that need to be considered. Legally he could request equal time. Especially as you've had sole custody since birth and you aren't disputing his relationship. Maybe you should discuss this with your solicitor before you meet with Morgan.'

'How do you know this stuff?'

'It wasn't all sweetness and light at home when I was growing up. The divorce was pretty savage.'

She knew the kids had been split up. Two each to the parents until their mum died and her two went to stay with their granddad. 'Do you miss the others?'

'No. I like being by myself. Win's the same.' He hung the tea towel on the rack with an air of finality. 'I'll be off now.'

She thanked him again but he didn't dawdle, the truck rumbling into life moments after he left the house. He'd given her plenty of food for thought.

She hadn't even considered the legal aspect, though she'd been the one to bring up the solicitor. She'd been thinking more about some kind of document stating he was legally their parent, though his name was on the birth certificates. She'd done it before Grace had come along with her proposition.

A small voice brought her out of her thoughts.

'Did you go and see Morgan?' Edward looked young and vulnerable in his superhero pyjamas.

'Yes.' She held out her arms and he came and climbed into her lap.

'Why doesn't he want us to be a family?'

Pain seared her heart. She'd hoped he hadn't read between the lines of what happened at the Hot Bread Shop. 'It's new to him. It takes a while to get used to. We've known the whole time.'

'He told Mr Field it wasn't true.'

'Mr Field is almost a stranger. They haven't spoken in years. You know we've talked about family things being private.'

His jaw set. 'He's ashamed of us. He's like Grace, keeping us a secret.'

How could she deny it? She couldn't reassure him because she had no idea what Morgan wanted. Only that he had no intention of marrying her to make a family.

'We're still talking about the best way to manage it. You know he likes you.'

'He didn't know I was his son. Gabby is the one he wants. Not me.'

Becca gripped his chin, forcing him to face her. 'Morgan spent time with you on your ships and bought you exactly the same present as Gabby, before he knew you were his.'

'So what?'

'It means he really *really* likes you. Not just because you're his son.'

Edward stilled, biting down on his bottom lip. 'Is that a good thing?'

'It's a good thing. Some dads might have ignored you. Might not like you. Especially if they think you have another dad.'

'Is that what your stepdad was like?'

She sucked in a steadying breath. 'Sometimes. He had a lot of worries because your grandmother was very sick.'

'Do you think Morgan wants to be our dad?'

'Absolutely.' She wasn't sure how it would play out, but she was sure of that much.

'Do you think he'd let us call him Dad?'

'I don't know. It's up to him. You'll have to talk to him about it.'

He was quiet for a moment or two. 'Why didn't he know about us when we were born? Didn't he want babies?'

'It's not his fault. It was Grace and I who decided not to tell him. It's hard work, studying to be a doctor, so Grace ... we thought it would be better to wait until he was finished studying.'

'It must have been a long time ago. He's old now. Not as old as Doctor Farrell, but older than the doctor who was working at the surgery when Doctor Farrell was sick.'

She wondered how Morgan would feel about that description. 'It was tricky. We expected him to come home and we were going to arrange for him to meet you.'

'That would have been cool. What happened?'

'He went to Africa and he stayed away for a long time. Grace and Grandpa Ned asked him to come home to visit but he was too busy. He had lots of children to look after over there. Lots of orphans who had no-one to look after them.'

'We had you and Grandpa Ned and Thackery and Grace.'

She couldn't help thinking Grace was an afterthought. Becca was almost sure the older woman loved the twins, but she couldn't seem to let herself show it and the twins were aware of a subtle barrier.

'Exactly. It was important work and we didn't want him to have to leave it and come home, though we wanted to see him very much.'

Gabby's sigh broke the tension. Becca had been aware of her hovering in the hallway. Maybe listening to the discussion would help her too.

Wandering into the room she went to the cupboard for a glass and poured herself some water, plonking herself down at the table. 'Dan's gone to bed.'

Becca waited while the girl took a long drink. 'Do you have any questions?'

Gabby eyed her narrowly. 'Were you and Morgan in love?'

'I loved him very much.'

The quick frown told her Gabby registered the omission of Morgan's feelings. 'Why didn't you get married?'

'It wasn't the right thing to do. We were both too young to get married. He was nineteen and at university. I was sixteen.'

'I worked it out myself from your birth dates. The same age as Kaylee was when she got pregnant with Craig.'

Surprised Gabby had known about Kaylee, she sat silent.

Gabby rolled her eyes. 'We aren't stupid, Mum. We do sex ed at school. I remember her going to school as big as a house. It wasn't that long ago. Everyone was talking about who the father was but no-one knew. I figured it must have been the same for you.'

'Didn't you want to talk about it?'

'Why? It's totally icky thinking about mums doing that stuff. I do know I'm going to wait until I'm at least thirty before I have kids.'

Becca stared at her daughter. 'Why?'

'Because it's not fair having to look after kids when everyone else your age is out having fun. I'm going to study and travel and make heaps of money before I think about boys.'

'I don't regret it.'

The girl's face softened. 'We know. You've been the best mum and the best role model.' She screwed up her nose. 'Except for the teen pregnancy bit. It's more like a ... a cautionary tale?'

Becca couldn't help laughing. Here was her twelve-year-old daughter talking life lessons. 'Why do you think I'm a role model? Except for the obvious.'

Edward twisted in her lap. 'You didn't let your mistakes stop you from doing your best. You studied hard and have a good job and we have everything we need.'

From laughter to tears in a moment. He was only reflecting back what she'd been saying to them for years. She hadn't expected them to apply it to her. She hugged him tight and he squirmed. 'Muuuum.'

She only held him tighter, beckoning Gabby to join them. When she had both of them in her arms, she squeezed hard and kissed them both on the forehead. 'You are the best thing that happened in my life. The best. Don't ever think I regret a single thing about having you.'

Gabby returned the hug. 'Well duh. Of course we know.'

They smiled at each other through happy tears. Despite the uncertainty of Morgan's homecoming, a new confidence surged through her. They would get through this, whatever happened.

***

'*Make it work.*'

Morgan stared at the poster of the human skeleton on the wall beside the door. He felt a strong kinship with it, though his body was starting to fill out. The muscle tone would take longer, a concentrated effort. He'd signed up at the local gym to have an assessment done and a program worked out to ensure he didn't overdo it.

In the meantime, he was mulling over the meeting with Toby Mallings. The solicitor had been helpful but he'd stressed the best outcome would be if they sorted the key areas between themselves before trying to wrap it up in a legal agreement. It would save money for a start. It would also save tying themselves up in the social security system. Something Becca had been determined not to do. But she'd have had experience of the system, unlike his own family who'd always been financially secure.

It hadn't been what he expected. Becca had seemed daunted by the ramifications of the decisions made twelve years ago. Toby had been amazingly patient with their questions. It was odd seeing solemn old Toby in business mode. Older than himself by a couple of years, Morgan remembered him as a stodgy boy with heavy-framed glasses, often the target of ill-natured jokes. They'd all grown up, something that occasionally startled Morgan when he met someone who had stayed in his mind as a teenager through the long years away.

When the solicitor had fixed both of them with his steely-eyed gaze from behind his frameless glasses and told them to 'make it work', Morgan experienced a new respect for the boy he'd remembered from long ago.

He and Becca had to work things out. She wasn't exactly enthusiastic. Not surprising considering she must have been smarting from his physical rejection last weekend. He tapped his pen on the desk. There were a few options. If he could only get Becca to put aside pride and accept help.

Checking the time, he calculated he had a few minutes before the afternoon influx of patients. Becca was in her office prepping the books for the accountant. The place ran like a well-oiled machine. He only had to concentrate on the medical side of things. Doctor Farrell had liked it that way. Morgan was itching to do more. This way he could focus on the expansion of the clinic.

He nodded to Laureen as he went past on his way to the Clinic Manager's office. The girl was eating a salad and leafing through a fashion magazine. Getting ideas for her next crazy hairdo maybe. He wasn't sure the faded blue suited her dark complexion, even if it matched the clinic uniform.

Becca's door was shut and he knocked, entering at her command. She looked surprised for a moment before her face settled into its usual passivity.

'How can I help you?'

He made himself comfortable in the chair across from her. 'We need to talk.'

She glanced at her laptop screen before closing it down. Folding her arms, she sat back. 'Go ahead.'

'This is not work related. I'd prefer meeting out of business hours. Could you come over tonight?'

'I have to finish packing up Dan's stuff.'

Morgan shifted. 'He's moving already?'

'They finished the building fit out earlier than initially expected. They want to get the tenants in straight away.'

'That's good, isn't it?'

Becca nodded. 'Better than delays. Dan doesn't handle anticipation well.'

'Do you need a hand to take his things down? I could loan you the car or drive you.'

Her lips curved up in a faint smile. 'It's all sorted, thank you. Thackery is taking him down in the truck, so he can take all his things with him.'

It had been like this all week. Since the kiss. She was polite. Courteous. But the rapport they'd started to build was gone. He missed it. He'd missed it for years.

'Is there much packing to do? Can I help?'

A flush edged her cheekbones. 'Not much. I could probably come over for a while if I can get someone to babysit.'

'I could ask my mother.'

The wry smile was back. 'Grace doesn't handle Dan's oddities. I'll get Thackery to come.'

'He doesn't mind the short notice?' He tried not to make it a question. It wasn't his business who Becca spent time with.

She tilted her head, studying him, her glasses catching the overhead light and obscuring her expression. 'He'll usually tell me if he can't. Most times it's okay. He's almost family.'

'How did you get to know him?'

'When the twins were small, he was still at school. He brought organic eggs and produce into town to sell every Monday and Friday and he'd drop off what he didn't sell on his way home at a cheap rate. He had this funny little trailer thing on his pushbike. I assume it was how he paid his way. Win never leaves the farm.'

'What about parents?'

'He never talks about them. I know his mum died.'

'So there's his sister and his aunty Beryl. Lucky him.'

They shared a smile at that image, Becca sobering quickly. 'He's not one to brood on the past.' She shot a pointed look at the clock.

The time was getting away. Fascinating as it was, he needed to make sure Becca would come. 'What time?'

'I'll check with Thackery, but after the children have eaten probably. I don't like to take advantage.'

Chapter 10

It was after eight when Becca headed up the hill to Morgan's place. She was starting to think of it as his, instead of the usual reference to the Maiden place. Before long the Maiden family would be consigned to obscurity, recalled only in a few place names and the dusty tomes of the local historical society. Most people from out of town assumed Maiden's Landing was something to do with a woman. No-one in living memory knew why the original explorers had named the watercourse Redemption Creek.

She entered through the back door where a light was on, pausing in the small anteroom to suck in a deep breath. She put up her hand to knock, only to have the kitchen door open wide.

Morgan stood there, holding the door. He wore a pair of jeans, still unfashionably loose from his weight loss, and an oversized grey V-neck pullover that showed the vulnerable hollows of his throat. He still had a long way to go to full health and a twinge in her chest confirmed she'd never stopped caring about him.

She stepped past him into the spacious kitchen, noting the half empty cup of coffee and scattered papers on the table in the centre of the room. 'Am I disturbing you?'

He shook his head. 'I was catching up on a few things while I waited. I'm not on call tonight.'

Half expecting him to return to the table, she moved over to a chair opposite the spot where he'd been working.

'I want to show you something.'

He went into the hallway and she followed, wondering at the way he'd blurted out the request.

She'd briefly seen the hallway and rooms last weekend, but he took her into each of them, turning on the lights. The bathroom was quite spacious, considering it held only a basin and a large clawfoot bath with an old-fashioned shower overhead. The separate toilet she recalled being tacked on at the back, off the small anteroom.

The three unfurnished bedrooms were all a good size and there were what must have been dressing rooms or storerooms attached to each, piled with boxes. In the surprisingly large dressing room off the master suite at the front of the house, there were a couple of old silky oak wardrobes matching the double bedroom suite in the main bedroom with its bare mattress and large bevelled mirror. It was a beautiful old house, only needing some TLC to bring it back to life.

Morgan halted in the large formal lounge room opposite the master bedroom. Like the bedroom it had a window seat set in a bay window that protruded onto the wide verandah. 'What do you think?'

'It's lovely. When it's all done up, it's going to be fabulous.'

'I had an idea after we were talking to the solicitor. About this house.'

He led her back to the side hall and showed her three more bedrooms, including his, the big sunroom that opened onto the closed in eastern verandah, and several smaller rooms. The place was massive. She suspected some of the smaller rooms nearest the kitchen had been servant's quarters early last century.

Finally they were back in the kitchen and she studied him curiously. Sweat beaded his forehead and he kept wiping his palms on his thighs. He was nervous?

'Are you all right?'

His smile was almost a grimace. 'I guess I'm anxious.'

With a jerky gesture of one hand, he indicated the chairs at the table and she sat directly opposite to the one he'd chosen.

He rested his forearms on the table, hands loosely clasped. 'I have a proposition to put to you.'

Becca wondered why he was making a meal of it. She wasn't stupid. He'd made his position clear. Even if she'd wanted it. *Who are you trying to kid?*

'*Okay.*'

'The house is too vast for one person. It's oversized for an average family.' He glanced up from his fingers and then away again. 'I wondered about splitting it into two residences.'

'I guess you could rent one out.'

'Not rent. I wondered if you'd like one part for you and Edward and Gabby. The main section at the front. I could have the section where I'm living at the moment.'

She opened her mouth to reject the idea but he held up his hand, palm out, quelling her.

'Please, let me finish.'

Clamping her lips together, she buried her fingers under her thighs to prevent herself from showing her reaction. She couldn't live so closely to Morgan. Not like this.

'I want to have the children as part of my daily life. You know the sort of hours I need to work. This way I'd see them naturally, without having to organise visitation rights and custody agreements.'

'I already have a place to live.'

'You could sell it and be free of debt. Use any profit to buy a car.'

That hadn't occurred to her. After the grind of the past decade, it would be nice not to have the mortgage hanging over her head. They could live very comfortably off her salary. 'How would it work? There's only the one kitchen.'

'I could put a kitchen in the narrow room off the sunroom and install a new bathroom in the small room beside my bedroom.'

'I thought you were planning to do it all up.'

She could see him visibly relax, as if her acquiescence was assured.

'That's the plan. Ensuite bathrooms and built-in wardrobes in the front bedrooms. Maybe a second one between the spare bedrooms in my section.'

'Soooo. This is a long-term plan? The moving in together thing?'

He shook his head, running long fingers through his short-cropped hair. 'There's no reason why it can't happen straight away. Once Dan has moved out, anyway. There's enough room for people to shift around when any of the renos require it.' He must have seen her doubtful expression. 'I could set up a temporary kitchen straight away with a hotplate and microwave etcetera. We wouldn't have to share at all. Separate entrances. I can use the side stairs once they're repaired. I have someone coming next week to fix all the stairs and the verandah rails.'

'You've put a lot of thought into this.' She spoke slowly, trying to read his expression. It could be ideal if it wasn't for the fear of betraying herself. How much would they see of each other anyway? She wouldn't have to escort them over to see their father. The children could pop back and forth as they wanted. 'Are you sure you don't want to restrict visits? Will there be a system where you'd let them know if they can't come over?'

'Why would I want that?'

'What if you brought a ... a date home?'

His eyes cooled. 'I don't think it's likely to be a problem.'

He'd probably go to his date's place. Sabine had a lovely house on the edge of town near the creek. Handy to town but private.

'Becca.' He gnawed his bottom lip, his brows meeting above his long nose. 'This is important to me. I've had so little of my children. I want to live with them. Not be the weekend dad who gets to do treats but none of the everyday things.'

And that was where it got you. Right in the heart. She'd had twelve years of her children, sharing all the everyday joys and sorrows. He'd had nothing.

'Would I pay rent?'

'No. You'd cover all your own living expenses, but I'd pay utilities and rates on the property.'

'What about the renovations? Who would pay for them?'

'My property, my expense.'

She folded her arms and his lip twitched. *Was she so easy to read?*

'If we benefit from the renovations we should contribute. If I sell the house, I should have some money to contribute, even after I pay out the mortgage and buy a car.'

Morgan was silent. She could almost hear his brain ticking over. Finally, he dipped his head. 'Agreed. I can contribute to Gabby and Edward's further education as part of my responsibilities.'

Becca had a strong feeling she'd been had. Knowing the Cavanaugh's idea of a college fund would be overly generous, he was probably going to top it up anyway. But it was his right to be a part of his children's lives. His right to contribute to the expenses. At least he hadn't attempted to take away all her independence by insisting on covering everything.

'In principle, I think it's probably a solution. I need to talk to Patsy at the realtors about what I can expect if I sell. Things would have changed in the last few years with all the new people coming into town.'

Morgan straightened in the chair, his eyes narrowing. 'I didn't realise it had gone as far as involving a real estate agent.'

'Years ago. Your mother thought it was a good idea for the kids and I to make a fresh start elsewhere.'

That triggered a tautening of his jaw. 'What did you think?'

'I was tempted. Aunt Bea was still alive then and she didn't want to leave town. She couldn't have cared for Dan by herself. The money for the property back then wouldn't have been enough to resettle us all.' She raised her palms into the air with a shrug. 'So, it didn't happen.'

The room was still then, Morgan seemingly absorbed in his thoughts. Not happy thoughts, if the furrow in his brow was any indication. It was something she'd become increasingly aware of these last weeks. His serious, almost sad demeanour whenever he was not engaged in conversation or focused on his work. Even then he was mostly sombre. Except with the children. For some reason, they managed to reach past his outer shell and bring him joy. He deserved to have the chance of being a full-time father.

'What happens if one of us decides to get married?'

The bleak look in his eyes struck at her resolution to remain distant. 'I've no intention of marrying. If you find someone to marry, we'd need to relook at the arrangements with the children.'

Something was going on here. Something beyond his reluctance to make any commitments beyond the children. That was understandable. It had been twelve years of living separate lives. He'd travelled the world and she'd stayed here, building a life for her family. The only thing they had in common these days were the twins. It wasn't necessary to be married to co-parent as Morgan kept reminding her. At times with an almost desperate air.

She pushed herself to her feet. There was a lot to process here, quite aside from the possibility of house sharing. If only she could bring herself to ask him more about this illness that brought him back home. Unwillingly. His reluctance to be here was clear enough.

'I should head home. Thackery always starts early for the market.'

Morgan rose in a hurry, following her to the door. They paused at the top of the steps and Becca checked out the large open area almost surrounded by sheds and the old stables. It would be a good place for the children. Morgan would be good for them. It meant keeping close to Grace and Ned. Something the twins would appreciate. They were fond of their grandparents and they had no other family. Although ... 'Jordan Taite is your cousin, isn't he?'

Pulling his attention back from the night sky, Morgan looked down with a puzzled frown. 'Yes. What brings that on?'

'I hadn't thought about it, but if you're acknowledged as their father, your extended family becomes Edward and Gabby's family. Cousins.'

'I've never had much to do with Jordan apart from family gatherings. He's closer to your age and we went to different schools.'

'All the same, it'll be nice for them to have more cousins. Susannah's little ones, too.'

A laugh grated its way from Morgan's chest. 'I don't know any of them. They've been married and had families while I've been gone. I've missed out on all of it. They're strangers.'

She recognised the pain in the bitten-out words. Not only his cousin's children but his own.

The momentary doubts about combining their households fled under the overwhelming guilt at what she had allowed to be stolen from Morgan. There was no way back. Only forward. Even if it hurt. She had a feeling that was a given in this situation.

*

Becca walked along the street to the clinic in a dream. She needed to get her head around what Patsy Maddox had to say about the property. No way had she imagined the kind of values the realtor had quoted at her. There was a potential buyer from Sydney looking for suitable residential waterfront land to build on as well. She shook her head. Events were rushing way too fast. In the eight years since her initial query, the changes in the town had sent real estate booming. All those tree-changers coming from the cities with surplus funds in their pockets from selling up at city prices.

There was no reason to pull back from Morgan's proposal. She could be quite independent and still let him have full access to the two children. It would be nice to not have to be the beggar at the gates. More like an equal partnership, with her being able to contribute her fair share. She almost skipped as she entered the clinic through the automatic door.

Laureen looked up from the computer with raised brows. 'You look chirpy. Come into a fortune?'

'Maybe.' Becca grinned back. 'I had my house valued.'

Karen ducked her head out of the medical storeroom. 'Good news?'

'Very good. Is Morgan in?'

Laureen waved at the closed door of the consultant's room. 'He's got Doctor Long in with him. They had lunch together and I think they're talking business.'

At that moment the door opened and Michael Long appeared. He was a familiar sight as he came up from Bialga a couple of times a week to operate at the hospital. His dark eyes focused on Becca and she returned his smile. Morgan emerged from the office and shook the other doctor's hand before the visitor left the clinic with a wave for the staff.

Morgan half turned, as if to enter his office and halted. 'Did you want to speak to me? I think I have a couple of minutes before the afternoon influx begins.'

Becca followed him in and sat in the chair at the end of the desk reserved for patients. 'I spoke to the real estate agent. She thinks I could get a good deal for my place.' When she named the amount his eyes widened.

'Impressive. I thought the riverside address might attract buyers, but the condition of the house would be against it.'

'She said it was an advantage. It'll be easy to bulldoze the place and start fresh. The only way it could be better is no house at all. People want to build something themselves to suit their lifestyle, apparently.'

He frowned down at the blotter on the desk, tracing the symbol of a well-known pharmaceutical company with the tip of his pen. 'What do you plan to do with the money, if you sell?'

'I'll get a car. Maybe a new one. Or pretty new. I can invest some for the children and a nest egg for me and some for Dan. Out of what's left some could go to the renovations.'

'You're still thinking of doing the house sharing?'

Something cold slithered down her spine. 'Have you changed your mind?'

'Of course not. With that amount of money, you'd have a lot more options. I wondered if you'd given any thought to what those options might be.'

'I thought we were doing it for the children.'

'That's what I want.' He settled back in the chair, flicking the pen around and around in those long fingers. 'At the time I proposed the plan, it seemed to be mutually beneficial. A financial boost for you in return for access to the children for me. It seems you don't need my help after all.'

Becca swallowed hard. 'It has nothing to do with money, Morgan. I could be a billionaire and still want to work out a way to co-parent with you that works for both of us.'

Did he seriously think he had nothing to offer apart from the financial incentive?

He avoided looking directly at her and she wondered if he resented her independence. Yet he'd been happy for her to cope with the usual expenses of running a family, only contributing to the accommodation.

Her thoughts were stalled by his sudden jerk to his feet. 'If you're happy to continue with the plan as we discussed, I'll go ahead with our arrangements. I'll let my parents know tonight.'

'Do you think Grace will approve?'

His cold eyes gave off a don't touch signal. 'It isn't up to her. She's no longer in a position to make those kinds of judgements. This is between you and me.'

Becca suspected Grace wouldn't see it that way. But the time was getting on and she gathered herself together and headed for the door.

'Becca?'

She stopped with her hand on the knob.

'What do you think of Michael Long?'

It took a moment to get her head around the abrupt change of subject. 'He's an excellent surgeon and I'm told he's a good diagnostician.'

'I'm talking with him about joining the clinic. He'll be able to take over a lot of the surgery and I can focus on clinical work once we have more patients taking up the opportunity to be treated locally.'

'I thought you were qualified as a surgeon.'

He flexed his fingers, attracting her attention to his hands. 'I can only do so much. It would work well to have someone to spread the load. He already does a major percentage of the hospital work.'

Once again she was wondering about his health. He'd already done a number of minor surgeries in the clinic and helped put Tory Dibble back together to ensure she could be safely flown to Sydney. He was more than capable.

She gripped the doorhandle. 'If you think it will work, it sounds good. He already knows the area.'

Morgan smiled at her like a teacher commending a pupil. He'd really wanted her approval for the change. It was a small thing, but it brought back the glow she'd lost at his less than enthusiastic receival of the news about her good fortune regarding the house.

Then she remembered he was telling Grace tonight about the plan to share the house. Settling into her office, she flicked open her laptop.

As Morgan said, it wasn't Grace's decision. It didn't mean she wouldn't have an opinion. And

Grace having an opinion usually meant trouble if it conflicted with anyone else's.

Chapter 11

Becca locked up the clinic with a feeling of inevitability. Today would be the first time she met Grace after Morgan was supposed to have told her of their plans last night. She'd broached the possibility with Gabby and Edward the previous night after the meal and they'd been ecstatic at the idea of living with their father, even in a separate part of the house.

Morgan hadn't been in today, having organised a locum while he travelled to Bialga for a specialist's appointment at the hospital and more meetings with people about the clinic expansion. She'd been tempted to call him to ask about his mother's reaction but chickened out when it came to it. They'd come a long way since he'd returned, but he was still keeping a noticeable distance with any personal relationship.

Her own feelings hadn't changed. Not in more than thirteen years. She'd loved him then, her childish adoration morphing into something more as she'd grown up, and her love was stronger than ever.

She'd wondered if seeing him would change things, but it had only confirmed nothing about her feeling for Morgan had altered. Nothing except the maturity of her feelings for him.

Grace tried to convince her it was the type of youthful infatuation that fades with the years, but deep in her heart, Becca had known differently. Her love overlaid years of quiet friendship and an understanding built on solid foundations. No matter the differences of years apart, that core of friendship couldn't be dismissed.

Morgan might have left it behind, but Becca could never forget.

How could she have forgotten him when she was confronted every day of the last twelve years by her children? Gabby, who was the image of him in looks, if not in personality.

She sometimes wondered if her daughter's friendly personality came from the Becca Walters who might have been if life hadn't pummelled all her self-confidence out of her. But it was Edward who carried the deepest imprint of his father.

The quiet determination, the shyness, the meticulous intellect. All those things she recognised in the youthful Morgan and confirmed in his fully-formed adult self in recent weeks.

How could she not love the man who'd gifted her with the two people she loved most in the world? How could she not love the qualities in him that she loved in her children? There was no way to extricate the two things, though she'd loved him long before her children were born.

The problem now, was how to make this uneasy alliance work for the sake of the children. Grace's passive hostility she could cope with, but Morgan's suggestion was likely to blow the uneasy truce out of the water.

She turned into the Cavanaugh driveway, noting Morgan's car parked beside his house. He was back from Bialga already. Ned was outside with the children, his tools out mending something on Edward's bike.

'I'm adjusting the seat and handlebars. They aren't quite right.' He dipped his head towards the house. 'Grace is waiting for you inside. She wants to talk privately.'

His sombre gaze reminded her of Morgan. 'Thanks, Ned. Fair warning, I take it.'

He shrugged and turned back to the task at hand. 'Fair warning.'

Conscious of Gabby's curious gaze, Becca mounted the back steps. If Ned was worried, it meant Grace was not happy.

*

What will people think?

Becca stared back at Grace, wondering why the woman was incredibly obdurate about anything that brought Morgan closer to Becca. She'd only just sat down at the kitchen table with a cup of tea when Morgan's mother went on the attack.

'It's not like we're getting married. It's a house sharing arrangement to enable Morgan to be a full-time father. I thought you'd approve.'

'People won't believe it's innocent. They'll think you're living together.'

Becca threw up her hands. 'What does it matter? Lots of people live together. Nobody cares.'

'People do. Morgan is a doctor. He's a respected member of the community. He can't be seen to be living...' She seemed to choke on the last word.

'In sin? Seriously, Grace. Even if it mattered, how many people will know?'

'The children will talk.'

'I imagine they will. They're thrilled at the idea they'll be living with Morgan, though we won't be living as a family. They love him.'

'People will judge him ... them. Doesn't that count with you?'

'I've been a single parent for twelve years, Grace. They've been "bastards" for all their lives. Do you think people are going to change how they look at the kids now, simply because their father is back in their lives and we aren't married? Nothing has changed. We are still the same people we were before Morgan came home.'

'That's the point. Morgan's reputation will be tarnished.'

'Because he's a single father not married to their mother? Join the real world, Grace. What century are you living in? Half the children in Maiden's Landing come from single parent families.'

'Don't exaggerate, Rebecca.'

'There are plenty and no-one thinks less of them for it.'

Becca's gaze was drawn to Grace's hands, the knuckles white as she gripped them tightly together. 'Can't we at least have the truth between us, Grace? It's been twelve years and you've never forgiven me. It's not about us anymore. It's about the children and what's best for them. You chose to deny Morgan years of his children's lives and I let it happen. It was supposed to be only until he graduated. Maybe four or five years. I don't blame him for being angry for missing out on twelve. I can't forgive myself, so how can I expect him to forgive me. You could have brought him back at any time. What I don't understand is why you let him come back now.'

'I didn't have a choice. He'd already organised it with Donald Farrell and paid the money out.'

'Did you intend to keep him away from here forever?'

There was a hot ball of something in her throat. Rage? Grief? Maybe a bit of both.

'I hoped you'd be gone. But you couldn't take a hint. I'd have paid anything you wanted to get you away from here. Instead, you settled in here like a burr under my saddle and then had to get a job working at the clinic. I knew if Morgan came back, he'd join the clinic. He talked about it years ago.'

Becca stared at her. 'I know you love the children. I know you love Morgan.' *Obsessively.* 'So it must be me you hate.'

Grace shook her head. 'I don't precisely hate you. Surprisingly enough, I've come to respect you. But I can't bear the thought of you and Morgan...'

'Me and Morgan? Why specifically me? He has to marry someone eventually.'

'He could marry Sabine Mallings and have a family with her. She's more our kind.'

'But Sabine can't...' Becca slammed her mouth shut.

What was wrong with her that anger with Grace almost made her share privileged information?

The anger simmered away. It had been years since she'd let herself get angry with Grace. But then they'd been focusing on the children. Now Morgan was back, Grace was back in protective mother mode.

'I'm not asking Morgan to marry me. All I want is for the children to be with their father. They've missed out on having him here through no fault of their own. Morgan's missed out through no fault of his own.'

'He chose not to come back here after he graduated. It was his choice.'

'It was your choice to let him stay away without giving him a reason to come home. You know he'd have come back for the children, whatever he feels about me.'

A flush stained the older woman's cheeks. 'I didn't want him to let the children influence him.' She flexed her fingers and flattened them on her knees. 'It wasn't fair. I knew he'd eventually marry. I didn't want it to be you. You had everything I wanted and it was easy for you.'

'Easy? You think it was easy?' Becca sucked in a deep breath. Hysteria wasn't going to help.

'Twins. You gave birth to twins and they survived. It made me angry. A slip of a thing like you could sleep with my son and get pregnant with two healthy babies and I couldn't carry to term.'

'You have Morgan.'

Grace smiled, her eyes holding a wealth of pain. 'The only one and he almost didn't survive. I don't like to remember how many pregnancies I miscarried before Morgan was born. Afterwards, I was too concerned with keeping him alive to consider more children. I was nearly forty by then, anyway.'

Becca struggled to focus on what Grace was trying to say. 'You lost a baby from a live birth?'

'Two. I was pregnant with twins.' Her cold eyes softened. 'They say it runs in families. I lost them at seven months.'

'Does Morgan know?'

She shook her head, a denial in her eyes before it made it to her lips. 'He couldn't know. It was before.'

'Before you married Ned?'

A silent nod confirmed the guess. 'Your great uncle Stephen. You won't remember him. He died long before you were born. Before I married Ned. A sickly family.' She said it like it was something learned by rote.

Becca stayed silent, shocked at Grace's sudden willingness to talk.

'I wasn't much older than you were when you had the twins. Stephen was a little older. I knew your father and Dan's stepfather when they were children. You'd remember your Uncle Blue.'

Grace should know she didn't remember her own father. Not properly. But Becca remembered his brother as being kind. Blue Walters was the sort of guy to marry a widow like Dan's mother to give her a home and her boy a father. 'I didn't know either of them well. Uncle Blue was away a lot working in the mines and then he was killed in that collapse that was on the news.' After which fifteen-year-old Dan started to go off the rails. Becca's stepdad was no role model and no-one had regretted him when he died soon after from liver failure. Grace was right. The whole Walters family was a disaster. 'I hardly remember my real dad.'

Grace acknowledged the snippet with a barely perceptible tightening of her lips. 'I suppose someone your age can't imagine what it was like back then. My parents didn't approve of Stephen but we were in love. Some puerile fantasy of being Romeo and Juliet.' The hardness was back in her voice briefly. 'Of course I became pregnant. My parents refused to let us marry and I refused to do anything else. I was sent away to stay with an aunt. They talked about adoption. In the end it didn't matter. They came early. The boy only lived a few minutes. The girl almost a day.'

Her heart aching, Becca searched for words. 'What happened with your Stephen?'

'He died while I was away. Fighting a bushfire in the hills. He had an asthma attack.' One finger drew a pattern on her knee. 'He hated people thinking he was weak. So he died.'

'I'm sorry, Grace. But what does it have to do with me? I'd have thought you'd be more sympathetic. Not less.'

'Every time I look at you with the children, it reminds me of what I lost. You look like your father and he looked like Stephen. Edward could have been my son.'

Becca remembered the first time Grace had seen the children, only a few days old. She'd hardly looked at Gabby with her quiff of bright red hair—the image of Morgan. She'd stared at Edward with a palpable hunger never repeated. Becca had thought at the time it was because Edward was male.

Grace kept talking, as if now the words were coming out, she couldn't hold in the torrent. 'It took ten years before I could bring myself to marry Ned. Another ten years before I managed to deliver a live child. For months we thought he wouldn't survive. I sometimes wonder if that's why he...' She gulped in the last of the words, the trickle petering out.

'Does Ned know?'

Looking up from her hands, Grace nodded. 'He always knew. We were neighbours.' She indicated the property on the opposite side to Morgan's place, extending off into the hills. 'He was older of course, but the Taites and the Cavanaughs always socialised. He was my partner for the Debutante ball because I wasn't allowed to go with Stephen. I never expected Ned to want to marry me. Not after what happened.'

There was a heavy silence, weighted with the emotions of this woman who Becca had dismissed as cold. The past exacted a heavy toll.

'What do you want me to do?'

Grace straightened with a pained grimace. Becca could almost hear her spine clicking into rigidity.

'Don't force Morgan into making decisions he doesn't want or need. If you live there with him, he'll eventually take notice of gossip and want to put it right.'

'I can say no, Grace. You know I can.'

'His health still isn't one hundred percent. Stress isn't good for him.'

Becca gathered her purse and jumper together. 'I can't promise anything. I will talk to Morgan about alternatives. Don't get your hopes up. I'm sorry if my presence in your life is painful, but you more than anyone know my decisions have always been about what is best for my children. Apart from one time when I allowed you to overrule me.'

As she walked across the paddock to Morgan's place, she focused on what she needed to say to him. She wouldn't be sharing the revelations about the past. Grace hadn't asked her to keep silent. She'd known it was unnecessary. They both knew how to keep secrets.

Chapter 12

Morgan's heart jolted at the sight of Becca in his bedroom. He'd half expected her but hadn't heard her arrive with his head under the old-fashioned shower with its noisy pipes.

She didn't move, her gaze fixed on the view from the window, arms wrapped around her waist, signalling her vulnerability. His bare feet on the polished timber floors hadn't been enough to alert her to his presence.

In a grey sweater and trackpants, she'd be feeling warm in the well-heated room. He knew what she was seeing from the easterly facing window. His whole family history was laid out in the view. Once upon a time the Maiden family owned the whole valley, this side of the river. Another branch owned the other side of town where the Smith's grazed their sheep.

Drought and a financial downturn in the 1890s brought on the first breakup of this property. A large swathe of land butting up against the mountains that went to the Harmsworth's and the Fleming's who later split part of their holdings with the Wilcott's. The first world war had taken Maiden senior and his three eldest sons leaving only a ten-year-old boy and his sisters. They'd sold a decent-sized parcel to the Taite family and a good part of the remaining land went to Ned Cavanaugh's grandfather when he married the youngest Maiden daughter. The French born Durand's took over the stretch on the town side of the Maiden homestead block around the same time, running cattle. It had left this small block of about thirty acres between the larger properties, most of it running back into the hills towards the national park.

The end of the second world war had seen the last sell off, the five-acre allotments along the river taken up by returned soldiers trying to scrape a living with market gardens utilising the water access. Only Becca's house still remained of the basic dwellings that sprouted in the post war decade. Most were sold off in acreage allotments and bulldozed to build more luxurious homes long before he'd left town. Becca's family was the only one to hold out and her grandfather Walter's legacy might soon be gone, funding a better future for her and her children.

This was the long, interconnected history which made his choice to go into medicine tougher than it might have been if there'd been siblings to take over from his father. The guilt had driven him for years.

'Becca?'

She didn't turn, hunching her shoulders further. 'I've been with your mother.'

'I suppose she didn't have anything positive to say.' His own confrontation with her hadn't been sweetness and light. The only positive thing was this time she hadn't overtly said anything against Becca. She was learning.

Becca huffed. 'Let's just say she doesn't think it's a good idea.'

'It's not up to her.'

'She resents me.'

Morgan would have liked to be able to deny it, but he knew his mother well enough to believe Becca might be right. She'd always had a thing about Becca's family. 'It's not her life.'

'Isn't it? She indicated quite clearly she'd rather see you marry anyone but me.'

'Marriage?' He sucked in a breath against the tightness in his chest. 'I didn't say anything about marriage.'

'I reminded her of what you said. She thinks if we live together, local opinion will force you into it.'

He edged further into the room, adjusting the bath sheet covering him from waist to calf. He eyed off the wardrobe where his clean clothes waited. 'Does it bother you? That people might talk?'

'People always talk. Only people like your mother and Beryl Harmsworth give a stuff about couples living together. I've talked to Gabby and Edward. They think it's a great idea. Of course.' There was an amused tone in her voice. At least his mother hadn't totally squashed Becca into submission.

'What do you think?'

'It's the best thing for the children. That's what counts. I don't want to upset your mother, but her hang-ups aren't my responsibility.'

He wondered what hang-ups his mother had revealed. 'I know she's overprotective. She's had good reasons to worry.'

Becca turned then, her eyes widening. 'Because of your health?'

He wished he'd gone and found some clothes before he'd engaged with her. Even the grotty ones he'd been wearing to clean the old storerooms.

'Morgan?' She circled him, staring at his bare skin like he was some kind of zoo animal. 'Is this why you had to come home from Africa?'

She halted in front of him, her hand reaching to brush against one of the lesions on his chest. Almost healed, but still red against his pale skin. Her touch burned and for a moment a twitch in his groin distracted him. Now it happens. With only a towel keeping him from humiliation.

Her eyes behind her glasses searched his body. 'I don't think I've seen atopic dermatitis like this in an adult.'

'I was run down. I've always been prone to eczema and the conditions over there exacerbated it. I was already scheduled to ship out when I caught pneumonia. It knocked me around.'

'At least it isn't contagious. The rumour mill had you with HIV or dengue fever at the very least.'

'Not contagious.' He lifted his hands. 'It's why I can only do limited surgery. The scrub chemicals are too harsh on my skin and I can't wear latex.'

'Gabby had some trouble when she was a toddler but it's cleared up. We still have to watch what soaps and shampoos we use.'

'Sorry. My bad.'

She smiled up at him. 'Edward has asthma from my side of the family. I guess we should have compared medical histories before we bred.'

The image of the two of them all those years ago hit him fair and square and a stirring in his crotch pulled his mind back to the present. Maybe she was remembering too because her eyes darkened. Her hand came out tentatively and stroked his chest, his nipple tightening under the cool touch. Like dry ice, so cold it burned.

Not only his nipple. He held his breath, feeling the other reaction he hadn't expected.

A crease appeared between her brows as she explored his body, touching the damaged skin with gentle fingers. Small bursts of hot sensation sparked with each press of her fingertips, zipping through his body and settling low in his gut.

'Do you have a cream to treat it?'

He nodded, indicating the tube lying on the bedside table. 'That's why I'm not dressed. I was planning on putting the cream on first.'

She twisted around to look at his back, her fingers gentle on his arm. 'Do you need a hand with applying it?'

Morgan shut his eyes. The fact that her touch in this situation was triggering a sexual reaction was all kinds of weird. He couldn't decide if it were good or bad. Her hands vanished, along with the heat they generated and he opened his eyes. Becca was studying the cream with her usual intense concentration for things medical.

She looked up, catching his eye and then away again. 'I'll do it. It won't take more than a couple of minutes.'

He subsided onto the stool in front of the antique dressing table, folding his hands across his lap. He could see her in the round mirror, carefully squeezing a fat slither of cream onto her forefinger. She focused on what she was doing and he was free to watch her, her pink tongue protruding from the corner of her mouth as she dabbed and spread in an ordered fashion from the nape of his neck, working down to the top edge of the towel. Very much the nurse.

It was the most sensual experience he'd had in years, her hands warm on his back. He couldn't remember when he'd last been touched like this. Been touched at all.

'Turn around.'

He obeyed her, spinning on the stool and parting his knees to allow her access to his chest, the towel drooping between his thighs. He could almost taste the scent of her, faintly floral with a hint of perspiration from the fleecy tracksuit. It was overlaid with the chemical smell of the cream, but he was used to that, hardly noticing it when more enticing flavours were feeding his soul. With his eyes shut, he could imagine this was about intimacy, her hands exploring his body, brushing his nipples into stiff peaks.

'Is that all?'

Her query broke into his daydream and heat flowed from his chest up his throat to blaze over his cheekbones. Opening his eyes, he met her gaze, soft and a little hazy, as if she'd maybe been dreaming too.

She blinked and indicated the towel. 'Are there some lower?'

He nodded, still confused by the sudden awakening. She started tugging at the towel and he was suddenly alert. 'No. No. I can deal with those.'

She reached past him to place the tube of cream on the dressing table, her breasts brushing his shoulder. Straightening, she picked up one corner of the bath sheet from close to his crotch, cleaning her hands on the thick towelling. Her gaze was on his face, but she had to have seen his body's reaction to what amounted to a massage. 'I guess that's it.'

But she didn't move. Her mouth wasn't far away with him seated and her slight build. Her tongue darted out again and his own mouth went dry. His body strained forward while the sane part of his mind told the other, more physical side, it would end badly.

He didn't care. After all these years, he needed, wanted to taste her.

He reached out and gripped her hips, bringing her closer. There was no resistance, only a speculative gleam in her eyes which were fixed on his face. She made first contact, leaning down to touch her mouth to his, sweeping lightly from side to side before settling it over his bottom lip.

Heat bloomed in his chest, firing his system into renewed life and he opened his mouth to taste her. He wanted to feed on her sweetness. Revel in her strength. Like some doomed vampire sucking life, drawing hope from her. She was everything he dreamed, warm and moist, tasting of mint, sweet tea and her own unique flavour.

Her hands stroked over his shoulders and down, bringing her breasts in the soft fabric against his chest. So good. He'd missed this. Missed her.

Sliding his hands up her sides, he broached the satin smooth flesh under the sweater and t-shirt. It was hot and a faint hint of moisture lay under the jut of her breasts. He'd wanted to explore her for weeks, to see what changes motherhood brought to her body. He stroked a thumb across the silky texture of her bra and she pulled away, yanking the top layers over her head.

For a moment she hesitated, looking down at his face, as if waiting for his reaction. The soft cups moulded her shape, her nipples pushing against the thin casing. *Beautiful.* He brought up both hands to lightly squeeze the tips and she shuddered, bringing her mouth back down on his with a moan.

He hardly remembered them moving to the bed, shedding clothes and bath sheet on the way. It was like their last time together, kissing and fondling for what seemed like an eternity, bodies melding together, hot and sweaty, the friction driving them both higher.

Her flesh appeared a rich honey against the pallor of his own sun-starved skin, her arms and legs tanned like her face. Her touch was the kiss of hot summer days, the brush of a spring breeze. Inside him a torrent of sensation blew away the chill of winter. It probably sounded crazy but it made sense in his head. Only she could be everything, all things.

He ventured to touch the curls at the juncture of her thighs and she arched into him, her mouth greedy on his, her hips pushing against the movement of his fingers as he delved deep, his thumb focused on the wet slickness at her centre.

A shudder racked her small frame and she squeaked out a protest, bucking against his hand. His heart beat hard against his chest and he knew what she'd expect next. His mind shifted and squirmed as he thought about condoms. His mother brought over all his stuff from his old room when he arrived, but he suspected a box of condoms last opened nearly thirteen years ago wouldn't be safe. He hadn't been expecting ... been prepared...

'Morgan, please.'

She was reaching for him, her hand exploring his stomach and lower and a cold sliver of dread trickled down his spine, chilling the warmth from his body. Stripping away the blood from his vitals.

Not now, please not now.

His hands dropped away and he rolled over, dropping his feet to the ground and turning his back to her.

'Morgan?'

The bed shifted and she was sitting beside him, huddling into a pillow.

'I'm sorry.' It was all he could bring himself to say. He shouldn't have tried, knowing failure was inevitable. Humiliating.

She looked confused, her eyes naked and unfocused without her glasses. With a wiggle that took her further away, she reached for where she'd discarded them on the bedside table.

'Did I do something wrong?'

She sounded young, so like the Becca of his memories it made his heart hurt. With her glasses on again, she scanned his body.

He reached for the towel lying in a bundle of Becca's clothes on the floor but it was too late. Her indrawn breath said everything.

'Oh...'

'It's not your problem, Becca.'

She was scrabbling on the floor for her clothes. 'It is. I shouldn't have. I didn't know. You should have told me you weren't into it and I wouldn't have...'

She stood in front of him, clutching the clothes against her chest.

Tears welled silently, magnified by the glasses and then shrinking again as they tracked down beside her nose.

His chest, his throat choked his voice.

With a muffled sob she spun around and her rapid steps echoed down the hallway, heading for the bathroom.

He let the towel drop and buried his face in his hands. She wouldn't be back. It was pointless him thinking of following her. There was nothing he could do or say to make it better. He'd been a fool to think a momentary surge of desire wouldn't be followed by the betrayal of his body. That because he wanted Becca so much, the emotional connection would somehow make things happen.

He was a grown man, but all he wanted to do was cry for the loss and the humiliation. His and, worst of all, Becca's. He'd hurt her again. She didn't deserve more pain.

He sucked in a stinging breath. He'd destroyed everything. If he'd stopped her before the kiss, nothing would have happened. After that disaster, she wouldn't want to face him.

All his plans, his hopes for some kind of family life, even at a distance were threatened.

Not threatened. Demolished. He couldn't stay and watch her turn to someone else. If he'd had something to offer her maybe it could be mended. But if nothing else, today proved he couldn't be a partner to anyone.

If he couldn't perform for the woman he loved, what hope was there of anyone else working out?

He was tired of hoping. Of wondering if he would ever be a man again.

Chapter 13

Becca faced herself in the spotty mirror above the basin in the old-style bathroom. She looked like death warmed up, all her colour drained, leaving her the same colour as her hastily donned trackpants and sweater. And tears. She never cried.

She'd been insane to think she and Morgan could live this closely. With her wanting him and him indifferent, it was a recipe for humiliation. She'd been almost sure he'd been at least partially aroused when she first kissed him. Yet a necking session where he'd sent her soaring left him cold. Which only went to prove any sexual desire he'd had for her as a teenager was long gone.

Scraping her hair back with her fingers, she splashed water over her face and tried to rub some colour into her cheeks. Her mouth was swollen and pouty from kissing Morgan and there was an ache in the pit of her stomach. Not to mention the nausea rising at the back of her throat. Only the first one would be visible to Grace when she went to pick up the children. It was almost dark, so perhaps she could hover at the door and avoid the well-lit kitchen.

Flicking off the light, she walked carefully along the dimming hallway to the back porch, slipping on her pull-on runners and letting herself out silently. It only took a few minutes to cross the open space to the fence separating the two properties. She could see lights on at the Cavanaugh place but Morgan's house remained pitch black. Anxiety stirred, and she wondered how upset he'd been by what happened. She turned away, finishing the short journey but hesitated at the bottom of the Cavanaugh stairs, seeking out the window of his room across the paddock. For a moment she thought something stirred in the shadowy frame, but no light pierced the darkness.

'Rebecca? What are you doing hovering around outside?' Grace's voice showed none of the passion of their earlier conversation. But the woman had a lifetime of controlling her feelings under her belt. Sympathy stirred at the memory of the woman's grief over her children, but the recollection of her resentment of her own grandchildren's existence stiffened Becca's spine.

'I think we're in for a cold snap. There's a bite in the air.' In more ways than one. But that was par for the course. She hadn't expected Grace to soften after the earlier revelations. Quite the opposite. People usually regretted revealing themselves to the enemy.

Gabby poked her nose out the door. 'How come you took so long?'

'I needed to talk to Morgan about Saturday night.' Not a total lie. She'd spoken to him yesterday briefly and she would have confirmed it if they hadn't been distracted.

'Is he coming with us?'

Becca nodded and an ache settled in her chest at the disappointment they were going to feel at the change of plan about the house. She hadn't said anything to Morgan yet, but he must feel the same way after her trying to seduce him and failing dismally.

Both children were ready to go, backpacks slung over their shoulders. Grace obviously didn't want Becca lingering. Maybe she was feeling a little exposed too. Becca sent them on their way, waiting until they were out of earshot before she spoke to Grace.

'You don't need to worry. We won't be going ahead with the house sharing scenario.'

If she'd expected Grace to show her pleasure at winning her point, the sombre response was a disappointment. 'I think it will be for the best in the long run.'

For who? The losers would be the children, but Becca had found the one thing she couldn't sacrifice for their sakes. Her self-respect. She fought too hard for it over the years.

Against the gossips of the town, the cool disdain of Grace Cavanaugh, and her own weakness.

*

It wasn't until Friday that Becca had a chance to speak to Morgan alone. Half the town seemed to have come down with flu, making for long hours in the surgery.

Morgan had meetings with Michael Long a couple of evenings; though he'd made time to go to the bistro with Sabine Mallings on the Thursday night according to the rumour mill.

No-one seemed to be linking him with Becca which she told herself was a relief in the circumstances. Karen mentioned a few people made comments about Morgan's resemblance to Gabby, but not in a nasty way. It seemed the town accepted Morgan's relationship with the two children without making a thing of it. For the locals who might have remembered Morgan and speculated it was old news and for the rest of the town, including the many new people, it was a matter of indifference.

Grace would be pleased.

Morgan was engrossed in something on his laptop when Becca ventured into his office after the last patient left. He glanced up as she sat down in the chair usually relegated to the patients. 'Half a moment.'

It was no hardship to sit and watch him, sketching in her mind the changes since he'd arrived home still recovering from his illness. He'd been steadily improving those first weeks, but this last week he seemed to have gone backwards, the bones on his face more prominent and shadows under his eyes.

Lowering the lid of the laptop, he shifted on his chair to face her. 'How can I help?'

'I want to talk to you about the house sharing thing.'

'Can't it wait until we're out of here? I'm free tonight.'

'I don't think it can wait. I've been trying to talk to you all week.'

His lashes fluttered as he lowered his lids to mask his eyes. 'What's so important?'

'I've taken my house off the market. The whole sharing thing isn't going to work.'

There was a stillness about him that reminded her of the kangaroos along the road near her place as they watched her go by on her bike, waiting to make their choice of which direction to make their escape.

'Any particular reason?'

'After what happened the other day, I thought you'd agree.'

'We made a mistake. One we can learn from for the future.'

He was cold. As if this was some kind of academic debate instead of real life where there were children who could be hurt and hearts that could be broken.

'I can't do it, Morgan. I can't live right next door where I'm reminded of what used to be and knowing it's different now. My place is close enough. The children can go back and forth easy enough, like they do with your parents.'

He was looking at the laptop, as if the answers might lie inside. 'So it's me that's the drawback.'

'I've had to put up with Grace's treatment for all these years. I don't need another person in my life who thinks I'm nothing.'

He jerked upright, pacing across the room to pause by the narrow examination bed. 'I don't think you're nothing. You've done an amazing job bringing up Gabby and Edward. I want to be friends. We need to be friends for the sake of the children.'

'And if I want more? If I want a relationship?'

His hand passed over his eyes, resting on his forehead, thumb and forefinger kneading his temples. 'You'll have to find one elsewhere.'

'I can't do that if I'm living in the same house as you. It wouldn't feel right.'

'Point taken.'

He looked down at her with something unfathomable in his cold eyes. 'I anticipated this and I've thought of a solution.'

Trust Morgan to think ahead. It proved she'd been right about his reaction to what happened. 'And?'

'I've been speaking to Michael Long about the possibility of taking over the practice if I were to leave. The locum who was here the other day, Jen Parker, is keen to find a permanent position which means she could join the clinic as a GP and Michael can continue his role as chief surgeon at the hospital.'

Her throat cut off her breath as she pushed herself to her feet and tried desperately to suck in air. 'You're leaving?'

So many thoughts bombarded her, she couldn't untangle them. 'Why?'

'It's obvious my presence here is the issue. I'm the alien influence causing disruption. If I remove myself, you can all go back to normal.'

'That's crazy. Your parents need you. Your children love you.' She indicated the office with a tremulous wave of one hand. 'You've barely started to get things sorted here. People are relying on you.'

Morgan straightened, his chin lifting. 'I have to go. As soon as I can organise a locum, I'll be leaving. Michael will be ready to take over at the end of next month.'

Becca wanted to reach out and grab him, as if that could stop him; but she knew better than to reveal any kind of weakness. She wouldn't give him that kind of power. She pushed her hands into her uniform pockets. 'What about the children?'

'I'll pay child support. They can contact me by email. Skype maybe. Visit where appropriate.'

'That's not the same as being here, being a father to them.'

'They managed for twelve years without me. The last few weeks were a mistake. I'm sorry.'

Becca searched his face. 'I don't understand. Talk to me, Morgan. Tell me why you're abandoning everything. Your parents, this clinic. Us. Your family.' With rare control, she managed not to add the emotive word 'again'.

'Not my family. Your family, Becca. I can't be a part of it. I can't marry you. It's a small town. They expect happy endings. As long as I'm here, they'll be watching. Talking. Wondering why.'

With a snort, Becca turned away, staring at the painting of a tropical jungle on the wall with eyes that saw nothing. 'Don't insult me with excuses. I'm not asking you to marry me. All I want is for you to be here for Edward and Gabby. They love you. They need you.'

'You want something I can't give.'

What could she say to that? Her heart screamed its need but he was going away again.

She'd begged him not to leave her once, all those years ago. He'd gone away and made sure not to come home for more than twelve years.

'It's not just about a relationship. I can live with the fact that you don't want me. I want someone I can rely on not to run when things get tough. For the children's sake.'

She could almost hear him clamping his mouth shut.

So. Damned. Controlled. What she wouldn't give to see him out of control just once.

Spinning on her heel, she turned to face him. His mouth was pressed into a thin line and his jaw pulsed with tension.

'Look, Morgan. You need to stay. You have your contract here. You're getting the clinic up to speed, you have your parents' health to consider. It's easier if we leave. We have nothing to keep us here with Dan gone. I can easily afford to resettle with what I'll get for the house. Maybe in Bialga.'

Something shifted in his expression, a bleakness in those enigmatic eyes. 'I wondered if the money from the house might influence your decision. I know how independent you are.' He flicked something invisible off his cuff. 'If you think moving is best in this situation I have no objection. I know you'd considered it before I came home. Naturally I'll give you all the assistance I can.'

'I don't need your help. I ... we ... don't need anything from you. I'll call the real estate agent and let her know the house is available if the buyers are still interested. They want to settle as soon as possible so they can clear the site and start building.'

He wanted to protest. She could see it in the flicker of a nerve on the side of his jaw. Instead he inclined his head. 'As you wish.'

She hesitated at the door. 'I suppose you want to cancel the Winter Festival launch tomorrow night?'

It took him a moment to answer, his expression oddly unfocused. 'No. No. We can go ahead with the outing. The children are looking forward to it. I'm sure we can be civil to each other for a few hours.'

Chapter 14

Morgan locked the car and pocketed the keys. Civility was overrated. You could freeze to death from civility. More so than the bitter weather that sent the temperatures plummeting along with the dense cloud cover. There'd been sleet earlier in the day but the afternoon had been overcast but clear.

The two children were bundled up in puffy jackets over tracksuits and wearing knitted woollen hats with earflaps extending into long braided tails. Gabby in her signature pink clashed spectacularly with her hair and Edward in a light blue. Becca wore her slightly shabby black woollen overcoat with green leggings tucked into fleecy boots in deference to the Christmas theme.

He'd gone to buy a ski jacket at the local drapery, his wardrobe lacking anything for this level of chill after his years away in warmer climes. Mrs Dibble, after discussing her granddaughter's condition at length, found him a bright red coat that clashed with his hair almost as badly as Gabby's pink. But it fitted and it was warm.

The two children were already dancing away, keen to join the celebrations in the park. Becca followed; her hands shoved into the pockets of her coat. The twins both wore gloves but she'd come out bare headed and with bare hands. He would have liked to offer her his pair but they would swamp her.

He'd miss her, miss them all. Pain stabbed at his chest, taking his breath.

While the two children grabbed their jackets, she'd informed him the buyer signed the documents of sale that morning, giving her until the end of the month to move out. Morgan hadn't expected things to move so quickly. He certainly hadn't expected her to tell him she'd be handing him her notice on Monday because she planned to get the children settled into their new school at Bialga for the beginning of next term.

Pulling his leather gloves on, he followed the small group, wanting to make the most of what was probably going to be the last family outing he'd be a part of.

After this, there'd only be occasional weekends with the children, depending on his clinic commitments and when he was on call. At least Bialga wasn't far away for picking them up. He'd been afraid she might go further, to Brisbane or Sydney or one of the other larger centres further away. It would have made visitation almost impossible, restricted to school holidays. Jeanette had been through it all with Tory's father. At least while the girl was in hospital she'd be able to see her dad, who'd moved to Sydney before Tory was born.

Morgan swallowed the ache in his throat. After the years without knowing he had children, and the hope of building something closer, it would have been too much to give up seeing them altogether.

The parklands glowed with the trees sparkling with lights. Down near the creek the reflections turned the scene into a fairyland. Gabby was enraptured, her eyes darting everywhere as they made their way through the crowds. His parents travelled in separately, intending to meet them near the bandstand at the centre of the park. They were almost there when a touch on his shoulder attracted his attention.

'Morgan?'

He halted and Becca and the children turned too, rushing to give Thackery a hug. He was wearing the fur-lined coat with jeans and sheepskin boots. His hair was tucked up into an oversized striped beanie in red, yellow and black. Morgan was starting to get used to the younger man with his passion for recycled clothing. Thackery would miss the children too and they'd miss seeing him.

Morgan pushed away a twinge of something in his chest that might have been guilt.

Had he pressured Becca into making a hasty decision she might regret? He'd regretted it the moment she'd announced her intentions, but how could he ask her to stay? She'd sold her home and there was no way she'd choose to live with him.

The two children were dragging Thackery with them towards the lovely federation era bandstand with coloured lights outlining the posts and the octagonal shape of the peaked roof with the finial on top. The sound of the local brass band tuning up was drawing the audience and Morgan found himself beside Becca as the movement pulled them forward.

Without thinking, he grabbed her hand, afraid he'd lose her in the surging motion of the crowd. She stiffened and then relaxed, allowing him to link his fingers with hers as they followed in the direction of the rest of their group. Even through his glove, warmth flowed from her touch.

Typically, Edward towed Thackery and Gabby to the front, immediately below the stairs. The moment they reached them, Becca tugged her hand from his, leaving him feeling chilled.

A local identity performed the welcome to country and once they'd finished the band broke into the theme music of a well-known soap opera. Tony Field jogged onto the stage looking every inch the star yet retaining that homegrown quality that reminded everyone here he was a local lad.

It was probably what made him so successful, taking that approachable guy persona into his role as the lovable larrikin in the long running show.

'It's great to be back at Maiden's Landing on the banks of Redemption Creek.' He went on to reminisce about his years growing up in town and his broad grin lit up the impromptu stage.

He made a great compere, announcing the local singers and the group of dancers from the ballet school with the same enthusiasm he brought to his appearances on television.

Edward was literally bouncing when his idol was introduced as an old buddy of Tony's. Perfectly true considering they'd been at school together.

Jimmy Maddox vaulted onto the stage with his acoustic guitar and a cheerful grin. He'd made his name locally doing covers of just about every major singer, both country and pop.

He was the featured artist for the event, along with Tony and their repartee between songs had the crowd laughing and cheering. Morgan was almost sure Edward was going to explode with excitement and Gabby wasn't far behind with her soulful worship of the soapy star. Finally, Maddox sang one of his new songs, a haunting ballad about lost love that dug into Morgan's chest. He glanced at Becca and saw her eyes mist up, a soft sniff quickly muffled in a cough.

A wisp of white flurried into Morgan's face and he put up one hand to touch the icy droplets. A murmur from the crowd grew into excitement as they recognised the snowflakes falling. Tony Field signalled the band and they broke into a Christmas carol, Jimmy leading the singing. It was the ideal segue from the sentiment of the previous performance. Soon the audience were singing along about snow and open fires and the mood shifted into the festive atmosphere as children ran around trying to catch the icy flakes on their tongues.

He spotted his parents taking cover under a picnic shelter and moved towards them, losing hold of Becca's hand again as she linked her arm with Thackery.

Soon they were in a huddle under the shelter of the awning. The twins stayed in the open, laughing and dancing with the other children.

Grace frowned. 'Should they be running around in the cold?'

Becca turned to watch them. 'They're enjoying themselves. We can bring them in shortly. I think the concert is about over.'

As she spoke, the singing finished and Tony was back on stage thanking the performers. A few announcements about upcoming events for the festival and the formal part of the night was over. People were dissipating, some to the bistro and cafés for meals or drinks and others heading for the carpark to head home. The snow had finished, leaving patches of ice and water over the exposed paths.

Thackery leaned close to Becca, pointing out someone across the park. 'I'll head over there. See you tomorrow.'

Morgan shifted closer to Becca. 'What's going on?'

'Amanda Tanner is out without her posse. Usually she has Marcia and Nicole and a couple of other girls with her.'

'Marcia's with Tony.' He scrutinised Amanda. 'I remember them now. From Dan and Ben's class.'

Becca looked around. 'I can't see the others.'

'What's with her and Thackery?'

'Nothing as far as I know. I think he supplies her with organic vegetables. She has this love hate thing going with healthy food.'

'Looks like she has a love hate thing going with Thackery.'

The woman had apparently reacted badly to whatever Thackery said and stalked off in a huff. She was having trouble maintaining her dignity with her high-heeled boots slipping in the wet snow.

Becca turned back as Grace mentioned her name. 'Are the children going to miss the snow once you move to Bialga?'

'We can always come up. It's only half an hour away.'

'Mum? What does Grace mean? We're not leaving.'

The accusing tones in Edward's voice couldn't be missed. He'd come up behind the adults, presumably bored with the snow. Gabby was heading their way too.

Becca sent Grace an accusing glance. 'I was going to tell you both tomorrow.'

'I don't want to go. I want to stay here with my dad. It's not fair.'

'Edward.' Morgan spoke with authority but the normally sedate Edward was boiling up a head of steam.

'You can't tell me what to do. You're all mean and horrible. Keeping secrets and being ashamed of Gabby and me. Hiding us. Now you want to send us away. I hate you. I hate you all.'

He spun around and ran off down the path, slipping and sliding in the slop left by the snow.

His mother bit her lip. 'I'm sorry. I didn't mean to upset him.'

Becca sighed. 'I knew they'd be upset. I wanted them to enjoy tonight before I told them what was happening. I better go get him. Gabby, you stay with Grace and Grandpa Ned.'

*

Becca was almost to the empty path along the creek when she realised Morgan was following her. 'Don't bother, Morgan. This isn't your problem.'

'He's still my son.'

Anger seared a hole in her chest. 'Is he?'

He was panting, trying to catch his breath and she remembered he was still recovering from pneumonia.

He bent over, gasping. 'Don't ... punish ... the children ... because I can't ... be what you want.'

'What is with you? I misread the signals. My mistake. I won't make that mistake again. Your answer is to put distance between us?'

'If you resent moving, you should have said so. I'm quite prepared to do it the other way.'

'Stop fighting. Both of you.' Edward's voice shattered the bubble.

Becca turned to him, remorse gripping her stomach. He stood on one of the picnic tables by the protective railing. The water was deep there, a bend in the creek undercutting the bank. A jolt of fear froze her in place.

'Edward, get down.'

'I hate you both. You don't care about Gabby and me. You keep fighting and now we can't live in the same town.'

Morgan moved sideways towards the railing. 'Edward, why don't you sit down? We're not fighting now. Come down and we can talk it through.'

Edward twisted wildly on the table, trying to keep them both in his sights. 'Go away. I don't want to talk. I want you to stop fighting.'

Becca kept her voice calm though her heart was racing. 'Sweetheart. It's okay. We can work it out.'

'No. You always say you can work it out but every time something good is going to happen you ruin it.'

'Is this about living with Morgan?'

'Yes. No. It's everything. We were happy before he came home. Now we know what it's like to have a dad, but you keep messing it up.

I wish he never came. It was better not knowing.'

Morgan's face was as pale as the patches of snow scattered on the grass. 'I know we've made mistakes. Give us a chance to do better.'

He was close now, only an arms-length away.

Edward skittered away and Becca was helpless to stop it. One foot slipped on a patch of melting snow and he went backwards, over the railing and into the icy water.

Morgan didn't hesitate, launching himself from the railing into the dark water. Becca was close behind kneeling so she could lean through the fence. She could hear the splashing and see a pale shadow in the water. Pulling her phone from her pocket she activated the torch, relieved to see Morgan dragging Edward to the jetty further along.

'Becca, call the ambulance.'

Fear made her clumsy but she managed to dial the emergency number. In moments she'd given the details and received the acknowledgement help was on the way.

Dragging herself to her feet, heart still pounding, she ran along the path to a safety gate, opening it wide as Morgan heaved Edward from the water and propped him in a sitting position. She fell on her knees beside them.

'Is he all right?'

'He needs his puffer.' Morgan sounded like he needed it too, wheezing almost as badly as Edward.

'It should be in his jacket pocket.'

Morgan rummaged in the pockets. 'Nothing. It must have fallen out.'

'I've got a spare.' She managed to pull it out of her shoulder bag and dropped it into Morgan's outstretched hand. Edward was panting, his lips going blue and she wondered if it might be too late. The chill of the water would have triggered the attack, his first for months.

Ambulance sirens screamed in the background and for some reason it brought back the last time she and Morgan faced a life and death situation. Brittany died and Dan had never been the same.

If Edward died...

'It's not going to happen.' Morgan's voice was rough with fear but he sucked in a calming breath, keeping his gaze fixed on his son's face. 'Breathe, Edward. Steady.'

He helped Edward with the puffer and there was a momentary relief in her son's eyes. They widened as he struggled to suck in another shallow breath and then another; the wheeze and tightness still there.

'Take off your coat, Becca.' Morgan dragged off Edward's jacket, dumping the saturated clothing onto the ground.

She yanked her buttons open in haste and wrapped the warm woollen coat around her son, careful not to restrict his breathing.

Morgan still spoke calmly, rubbing Edward's back under his clothes and encouraging him to breathe. For all her confidence in him as a doctor, the arrival of the paramedics with their equipment eased her fear. In moments Edward was on oxygen and a nebuliser was being prepped.

Morgan handed her the car keys. 'I'll go with him in the ambulance and we'll meet you there.'

She started to protest but he closed his hands over hers with the keys. 'I promise I'll look after him until you arrive.'

She'd thought she'd have to search for Gabby and Morgan's parents, but the sound of the ambulance had attracted a crowd. Gabby darted out from under Grace's hand and flung herself at her mother. 'Is he okay?'

'He'll be fine. We need to get to the hospital.'

Grace nodded, her face almost as pale as Morgan's. 'We'll come too and bring Gabby. You go on ahead in Morgan's car.'

Gabby looked like she might argue but Ned took her hand. 'Your Mum needs to get there fast and you won't be able to see Edward straight up.'

With a silent thank you to Ned, Becca ran to the car and managed to steer the brute of the thing to the hospital, pulling into the doctor's designated carpark.

Inside, one of the nurses recognised her and pointed the way.

She arrived to find Edward sitting on a bed in the emergency bay, breathing steadily. Morgan was checking his obs, still in his wet clothes minus his jacket. The blue was fading from around Edward's mouth and nose and she steadied herself as a wave of dizziness brought spots before her eyes.

'Breathe, Becca.' One of the nurses patted her on the shoulder. 'You've been rushing and probably hyperventilated.'

Sitting on the hard vinyl chair in the corner of the bay, Becca did as she was told. She'd be no use to anyone if she collapsed.

Morgan came over a few minutes later. 'I'm going to admit him overnight, just for observation. The water was icy and his body temp is a bit low. He's already on the mend.'

He was reassuring in doctor mode, the soothing words washing over her. He'd been incredibly calm, even though it was his son.

'I'm glad you were there. I don't think I could have got him out of the water.'

He smiled crookedly. 'You might be surprised. Mother love is a powerful adrenaline boost.'

She reached out and pressed a palm against his wet shirt. 'You need to get changed or you'll get a chill.'

'Yes, mother bear.'

His eyes were soft for the first time in a week and she needed that reassurance. 'What happens now?'

'We'll get him into a ward. You head back to the waiting room. I'm sure Gabby and my parents will be desperate to know how he is. Once he's settled, you can come up and tuck him in for the night.'

Chapter 15

Gabby was pacing the empty waiting room when Becca entered, changing direction as soon as she spotted her.

'How is he? Will he be all right? Did they have to put him on a nebuliser?'

Becca leaned into the tight hug her daughter gave her, grateful for everything. 'He's much better. Yes, he'll be all right and yes, he needed a nebuliser.'

She sent the girl with some money to get snacks from the vending machine near the reception desk.

Grace had an almost vulnerable expression on her face, perched on the edge of one of the hard plastic chairs with Ned sitting beside her looking tired. 'I'm sorry I upset him.'

'It was bound to happen. I knew they wouldn't be happy with the decision.'

'I don't understand. Why go now, after all this time?'

Becca raised a brow. 'I thought you'd be pleased. It's what you've been pushing for long enough.'

'It's different now.'

'I don't see how. You still don't want us in Morgan's life.'

The older woman bit her lip. 'I never thought about the alternative.'

'My taking the twins away?'

'It wasn't until you started talking about finding someplace else for the children to go after school that I realised how much I was going to miss them.'

'You've grown accustomed to their faces?'

Grace wrinkled her nose. 'There's no need to be sarcastic, Rebecca. Ned and I have always been fond of the children.'

'It's me you can't stomach. Apparently, it's like mother, like son. I can put up with one Cavanaugh despising me, but two is more than I can swallow.'

Ned shifted in his seat. 'Why would you think Morgan despises you?'

Heat washed up Becca's throat and Ned nodded, his eyes kind.

'It's no use, Ned. The decision's been made. It's too late to back out now.'

'I understand the sale is final, but it doesn't mean you can't compromise.'

'I've spent too many years compromising. It's time for me to make a fresh start, and I can't do it here.'

Gabby leaned over the back of one of the rows of chairs in the middle of the room, a drink in one hand. 'Why can't we stay here?'

'Because it wouldn't work. We need to make our own life, instead of relying on Grace and Grandpa Ned.'

'What about Morgan? He wouldn't want us to move away. He likes us.'

How could she tell her daughter it wasn't about his feelings for the children?

Gabby tossed the empty drink bottle into the waste basket. 'It's because Grace doesn't like us, isn't it?'

She should have known Gabby would add up the pieces. 'That's not true.'

'Isn't it? Or is it you she doesn't like?'

A stifled sound came from Grace.

Gabby spun around to face her grandmother, who'd come to stand beside Becca.

'It's your fault we have to go away, isn't it? It's not fair. I know you don't like us much and you wish Dad married someone else and had some other grandchildren so you could love them. I know you're sad about your babies, but it's not Mum's fault. It's not right for you to punish us because of something that happened a long time ago. Would it make you happy if Edward died?'

Grace paled. 'Of course not. How do you know?'

'I came inside to wash my hands while you were telling Mum about them. I'm sorry your babies died. I'm sorry we make you remember how sad it makes you. But it's not Mum's fault. You don't have to love us. Mum says you can't force people to love you. But you don't have to be mean to them.'

Grace sat heavily. 'Oh, Gabby, I'm sorry. I never meant you to feel unloved.'

Folding her arms over her thin chest, looking disdainfully down her long nose, Gabby bore a strong resemblance to her grandmother. 'You meant to make Mum feel bad though, didn't you?'

Becca reached out to pull the girl away. 'Gabby, no.'

Grace shook her head. 'Let her talk. It's probably about time we cleared the air.'

'It's not the time.'

The older woman snorted. 'Isn't that my line?' She glanced over at Ned, who sat quietly, a pained expression on his face. 'Nothing to say?'

He shook his head. 'When have you ever listened to me, Gracey?'

'No. You're right. It always had to be my way. You could have stopped me, Ned.'

'Could I? It never looked that way. Not even when we first married.'

Something softened in her face. 'Why?'

'It seemed like marrying me was something you did against your will. I couldn't ask for more.'

Gabby moved over to drape her arms around Ned's shoulders. 'I'm sure Grace loves you, Grandpa Ned.'

His silence spoke loudly in the small room.

Grace shifted in her seat. 'You doubted my love for you?'

'You were all wrapped up in your grief. You told me you couldn't bear to love again, but you wanted children. I couldn't give you what you wanted. Only Morgan and he was a frail baby. You were always fretting about him, even when he seemed stronger. I suppose I guessed you blamed me.'

Tears pricked Becca's eyes, and for a moment, an echoing gleam sparked in Grace's bleak gaze.

'It seems Gabby was right. I've been trying so hard not to love people I've ended up being mean to them.'

'You never treated the children badly.' *Even if they didn't feel loved.* The unspoken words hung in the air.

'I treated you badly and through that, I hurt them. I never thought about what they might think about my attitude to you. They love you; of course they resented my treating you like you were a thorn in my side.'

'They aren't stupid, Grace.'

'No. I was proud of them. Thinking they took after Morgan. I didn't want to see how much they took after you. Gabby has a fine sense of justice. I suspect that comes down to your upbringing.' Grace swiped a tear from her cheek and Gabby popped up, holding out the box of tissues from the coffee table.

'You're a really good cook, Grace. I'm sure if you decided to be a good grandmother, you could be good at it. If you wanted.'

Mopping her suddenly damp cheeks, Grace shook her head. 'It's too late. How could you forgive me for what I've done? I kept your dad away from you.'

'Well, Mum says even though it's hard to forgive people who hurt us sometimes, we can pretend and then it comes easier. Eventually it can be true.'

Grace laughed, a raw sound choked with tears. 'You know how to stick the knife in, don't you, girl?'

Gabby sat on the chair beside her, her grin wicked. 'We do take a bit after you too. Would you like to be our proper grandma?'

'I would. Do I have to be called Grandma though?' Her expression was eloquent. Grace was still Grace, after all.

Gabby slipped a slender arm around the older woman's shoulders. 'We're used to calling you Grace.'

The two hugged and Becca found herself holding back tears. If nothing else, at least something was mended tonight.

Ned stood, rolling his shoulders to release the stiffness. 'We should be going home, Gracey.'

It seemed odd to hear the affectionate nickname coming from Ned. But Grace seemed to respond to it, a soft flush on her cheeks. 'Of course. It's late.' She smiled down at the girl leaning against her. 'Would you like to come home with us? Your mum is likely to be here for a while.'

Gabby nodded, sliding her hand into her grandmothers with a firm statement of trust. 'Do I get to sleep in Dad's old room?'

'If you like.'

'Awesome.'

Becca bent to kiss her as they went past.

Grace seemed unusually awkward. 'You can come over tomorrow whenever you're ready. We'll take Gabby to church with us. At some point we should have a proper talk.'

Between them was the last talk that had been painful for both of them. Becca smiled, pushing aside the ache in her chest.

'I'd like to talk.'

Becca had scarcely sat down again when Morgan appeared from the hallway leading to the wards. He'd changed from his wet clothes into scrubs, the pale blue accentuating his eyes. The short sleeves left his arms bared and she could see patches of discolouration in the delicate skin inside his elbows. It reminded her too clearly of his lean body exposed for her the other night. And what came after.

'How is he?'

'He's doing well. Come along and say goodnight.'

She followed him along the corridor and into the acute ward nearest the nursing station. 'I thought he'd be better here as there aren't any other children in at the moment. They'll do regular obs to make sure the immersion didn't have any aftereffects.'

Edward was still partly propped up in due regard for his condition, but she could see he was sleepy. Exhausted after the trauma of the evening.

She sat beside him and rested her hand on his wrist, careful not to disturb the pulse oximeter on his middle finger. 'Hey.'

'Hey, Mum.' His voice was thready but some of it was probably due to tiredness.

'They treating you well?'

He grinned sleepily at her. 'Of course. Will someone check Kirsty?'

'Thackery is taking her up to the farm for Win to look after.'

'She'll like that.'

Becca wondered which one he meant. Probably both. 'You okay if I go home or would you like me to stay?'

'You go. I'm gonna sleep forever.'

Already his lids were drooping and she leaned over to kiss him. 'I'll be back first thing.'

'Goodnight, Mum ... gunnight, Dad.'

She sat with him for a few more minutes but he was out to it, his breathing deep and even.

Morgan touched her on the shoulder. 'They'll monitor him all night. If there are no further symptoms, he can come home tomorrow.'

A numbness was overtaking her as she followed Morgan out of the ward. A male nurse met them at the emergency room with a bag holding wet clothes and her coat in a separate bundle. She pulled on the coat, knowing it was still freezing outside, even if the snow had stopped. It was still clammy from being wrapped around Edward, but better than nothing. Which was more than Morgan had.

'Are you going to be all right?'

The nurse told them to hang on a minute and vanished into the ER, coming back with a black puffy ski jacket. 'You can use this. I have another one in my car.'

Morgan thanked him and Becca watched the nurse head off. 'That was nice of him.'

'More likely he didn't want me rolling up on his shift with pneumonia.'

She smiled at him and his eyes widened, the blue startlingly bright under the hospital fluoros. He took her elbow and steered her to the exit.

'We need to get you home. Another big day tomorrow.'

She didn't argue when he took the car keys from her. A ten-minute drive was not going to kill anyone. Especially when Morgan turned up the heater in the car. It was lovely, nestling back into the comfy leather seat and watching the headlights pick out the patches of white snow along the edge of the road.

The evening had been lovely until the disaster with Edward. Like a real family outing. It was hard to remember they weren't a proper family sometimes. At least once they were out of his hair, Morgan would be able to think seriously about his own future.

'I didn't see Sabine at the festival.' She cringed inside at the way the words spilled out.

Morgan glanced across. 'Sabine's in Sydney for the holidays. She's taking schoolwork down for Tory Dibble so she doesn't get behind while she's in hospital. I had to see her the other night to finalise the arrangements.'

'That's why you've been seeing her?'

'Jeanette was worried about it. Sabine has been helping me liaise with the hospital in Sydney. They have a school attached to the Children's Hospital for long-term patients.'

Becca looked back over the events of the past weeks with new eyes. 'That's the only reason?'

'I'm not dating her. I told you I'm not in the market for a relationship.'

He sounded tired. As he should be after having to rescue Edward.

'I thought you meant with me. Grace seemed to think...'

'We know what my mother thinks. The Mallings' are old money and naturally she looks at Sabine and thinks purebred little aristocrats.'

She couldn't help laughing, though there was an edge of truth in the words that stung. 'She seems to be changing her mind. I always wondered if she loved the twins or whether it was the price she had to pay for keeping me out of your life.'

'It's time we talked about those reasons.'

They were turning up his driveway before she realised where they were heading and she twisted to look at him. 'Aren't you dropping me home?'

'For a start, I think you're better off not being alone. You've had a bad time and could be suffering from shock.'

'And the rest?'

'I need to talk to you. About my mother.' He compressed his lips as they pulled into his garage. 'I need to explain about what happened back when the babies were born.'

'What happened? I thought we'd settled everything.'

'I'm pretty sure you think my mother's pressure on you was unfair. There was more going on than you probably realise.'

'Like what?'

'I'm not going to freeze to death in a car while I narrate a long and rather tedious story. I'm cold and I need a hot shower to get warm again. You need one too. Your hair is wet and I'm pretty sure your clothes are still damp.'

He climbed out of the car with this last pointed comment and she did the same, huddling into her coat. She was still cold and damp from the snow and holding Edward while she'd put her coat around him.

She stumbled as her boots hit the rutted surface of the yard and Morgan steadied her. 'I'm sorry I can't do the macho thing and carry you inside, I'm still wiped out from pulling Edward out of the creek. He weighed a tonne with his waterlogged clothing.'

'It's okay. I didn't see the rough ground. My glasses are a bit fogged up.'

All the same, he guided her into the house and to the bathroom. 'You go first. I'll put the kettle on and make sure the radiator is on in the bedroom.'

He grabbed a couple of towels from the old-fashioned linen press and indicated a navy dressing gown on a hook behind the door. 'You can borrow my robe until we dry your clothes.'

She was already in the shower with the hot water pummelling her aching body when she remembered he'd said bedroom.

Singular.

Not that it mattered. Morgan wasn't into her. She might have been a bit slow, but the second time was the charm.

With a towel wrapped turban wise around her hair and swamped in Morgan's fleecy robe, she gathered up her clothes and headed towards Morgan's bedroom. The sound of a kettle bubbling halted her at the kitchen door and she stared at him, still in the scrubs, the borrowed jacket hanging over the back of a chair. He leaned on the bench, his head bowed, sucking in deep breaths.

'Are you all right? Did you get your chest checked out while you were there?'

He spun around, his hand brushing over his frowning face, as if she'd woken him from some dark nightmare. 'My chest? No, it's all right. Jen Parker was there and she ran her stethoscope over me once Edward was stabilised. I'm aching a bit from the physical exertion. Nothing serious.'

'We don't have to do this tonight.'

'Yes, we do. It's obvious the twins are picking up on what's been going on. They need us to make things work.'

'I don't see how revisiting the past will make any difference.'

He passed his hand over his damp hair. 'I would prefer to have this discussion after a hot shower with a warm drink to get rid of the chill of the damn creek water.'

Becca clutched the clothes to her chest. 'Of course. Do you want me to make the drinks while you're in the shower?'

He nodded, coming towards the door. 'Kettle's boiled. Milk is in the fridge and the rest of the makings are in the cupboard above the jug.'

He passed her, being careful not to touch and she went through to the sunroom to hang her clothes and the ones in the bag on the rack he had set up in what would normally be a sunny corner.

By the time the noise of the shower stopped, she was in his room, a tray with two mugs of hot chocolate and a plate of Anzacs on the chest at the end of the bed. There was nowhere to sit apart from the bed, but it was the warmest room apart from the bathroom and the kitchen itself, the radiator connected to a wood stove that ran the hot water system and sent boiling water throughout the house.

Only a handful of rooms had the heat turned on, but it would have warmed the whole house beautifully if she'd brought the children here.

Pain lanced through her at what she'd given up for the sake of her pride. She shouldn't have punished the children for her own inadequacies. She should have listened when Morgan told her he didn't want a relationship.

After all this time, it seemed she'd lost the ability to interpret his body's signals, reading sexual attraction into what was simply an attempt to build a friendship to enable them to co-parent.

None of it explained his impulse to run. But then he'd been running for thirteen years.

She studied him as he came into the room, wearing a pair of clingy knit boxer shorts and a loose t-shirt he must have found elsewhere in the house. Maybe the laundry. The patches of red on his arms and legs were fading. On most people you would hardly notice them, but his clear pale skin with the tinge of blue veining showed everything. Despite being underweight, he looked good, all lean muscle and broad shoulders.

Her study of him reached his face and hot colour surged under her skin at the raised brows and almost pained expression on his face. This was not going to go well. Unless she could control her stupid lust.

It would be easier if she could stop caring, but the caring seemed to be permanently ingrained.

Chapter 16

Becca Walters on his bed. Looking like he was her favourite kind of chocolate cake.

A frisson of something ran down his spine. *Not going there.*

He moved the tray from the blanket chest to the bedside table and grabbed a couple of extra pillows, tossing them onto the bed. 'Prop yourself up against the bedhead and we can talk while we drink.'

She squirmed into place, hastily adjusting the robe when it fell open to reveal her legs and gaped at the neck. This would be easier if he'd managed to kill his emotions as well as his libido. Although his body wasn't quite as dead as it once was. But still not reliable. Not enough.

He planted himself at the end of the bed after passing her a hot chocolate. She refused the biscuits, but wrapped her hands around the mug, blowing on the surface.

'Comfortable?'

He kept one foot on the ground in best golden age Hollywood fashion, the other one hooked in front of him, keeping him steady.

Becca sipped at the chocolate and wrinkled her nose. 'What's this all about?'

He studied the milky bubbles on top of his drink. 'I was hoping not to tell you this, but I think in the interests of a better understanding for the sake of the children, I need to come clean.'

She had her game face on, unreadable apart from the sudden flutter of lashes quickly controlled. 'About?'

He leaned forward to place the mug down. How was he going to explain this without blurting it out baldly?

Shame still made his tongue clumsy. 'Do you remember when I told Mum and Dad I didn't want to work the farm?'

Becca rolled her eyes and suddenly the resemblance to Gabby was there, more in expression than features. 'Grace nearly went ballistic.'

'We came from a long line of farmers and I was the only son. Going into medicine involved an immense sacrifice on their part. The knowledge there'd be no-one to carry on after umpteen generations.'

'She's happy about you being a doctor.'

'It took a long while for her to come around, but it made the pressure greater.'

'What did your father think? I never quite figured it out.'

'He was caught between a rock and a hard place. If he encouraged me it would upset Grace, if he didn't, he'd betray all he believed in as a father. He was disappointed, of course. I think he hoped one of my children might be interested in farming as a career. Not that it's easy these days.'

'I don't think Gabby and Edward are interested, but that might change. You could have more children.'

The blow hit deep in Morgan's gut. This was why he had to be upfront. Her assumptions were painful and he tended to hit back. A clearer understanding had to be the first priority. Then, they could work out the best way of doing things without having to bring in the lawyers.

Her eyes narrowed. 'What does this have to do with the children and us leaving?'

Placing his hands on his thighs he forced himself to say the words that would start things rolling. 'It ties in with what happened after the accident. When Brittany died.'

He didn't need to be looking at her to hear the indrawn breath but she didn't speak.

'After that night, I had a ... a crisis of faith. I'd asked my parents to sacrifice the future of the farm, and I couldn't save a girl's life when it mattered. She was young and pretty, and a genuinely nice person. It didn't seem fair. I thought if I was going to ask my parents to give up any hope of me farming, if a young woman was going to die when I should have been able to save her, I needed to do better.'

'It wasn't your fault, Morgan. The coroner's report said the brain damage was too much. If she'd lived she would have been...' She stumbled to a halt, not saying the words trembling on her lips.

Dan's brain damage must have been tough enough to deal with. The bright and sparkling Brittany lingering on in a vegetative state would have broken the town's heart. It would have been worse than her tragic death.

'I know it all, in my head. Looking back. At the time it felt like a massive failure on my part. I imagined if I'd been better, studied more, I could have changed the outcome. I threw myself into my studies, working way too hard and not achieving anything. I couldn't eat, couldn't sleep. I ended up failing two subjects and just scraping through the others.'

There was a cathartic pleasure in letting it all out. If he and Becca hadn't broken up, maybe he would have been able to talk it through. She'd always been his sounding board when he couldn't share with his parents. Maybe things wouldn't have got to the stage where his parents needed to pick him up off the floor and force him to seek medical help. She was gripping the mug, but her eyes were on him, wide and full of sympathy. He'd missed her in those months before his collapse. He'd missed her every single day since. He hadn't registered she'd been his best friend as well as lover until he'd lost it all.

Her brow creased. 'Was that in the same month the twins were born?'

'Mum came down to see you after you called her. I knew nothing about it at the time. She told me recently.' He'd managed to get the full story from her, hoping he wouldn't have to expose his weakness to Becca. It was no use. Only the whole truth mattered now. 'What she found was a mess. The apartment was a mess, but I was more so. I could scarcely function. It was a breakdown, caused by stress and a bit of PTSD from my involvement in the aftermath of the accident.'

'Oh, Morgan, if only I'd known.' Her hand reached out to touch his knee and he flinched automatically. She instantly withdrew and he struggled to control his immediate urge to grab her hand and hold it.

'You had enough on your plate. If I'd been healthy enough to have been told the truth it might have worked out differently. They all ganged up on me—Mum, the doctors, my tutor at uni. I had a couple of nights in hospital on suicide watch.' He regretted his honesty when she winced.

'I didn't try anything. They were overreacting.'

'Were they?' She sounded doubtful but with her family history, it was probably normal.

'They released me into Mum's care and Dad came along for a holiday on the coast. Total relaxation. I was bombed out on medication. Even if I'd wanted to think, my brain would have rolled over and played dead.'

Her mouth quirked at the wry humour, but her eyes still had a deep sorrow he'd hoped never to see.

'I knew you'd had a baby. We ran into Jeanette and Tory on holiday and she mentioned you'd given birth and gone to Brisbane. Mum pretended not to know anything when I asked.'

'Jeanette wouldn't have known they were twins straight away unless she was talking to someone at the hospital. I think Doctor Farrell was worried about Edward being frail so he told the staff to keep quiet.' She smiled crookedly. 'No point trumpeting about twins if they didn't survive.'

Guilt swamped him. He'd been so self-absorbed he'd let himself fall into depression and been unable to focus on anything but his own health for years.

Even with his parents' help, it couldn't have been easy for a teenager having to cope. All the things his psychologist and doctors told him flooded his mind. It wasn't a conscious choice. He probably couldn't have avoided it under the circumstances. All the supposed reassurance they'd drummed into him. But he'd made a lot of poor choices which helped push him beyond his limits. The worst of which was abandoning Becca because of the word of a boy he knew to be an addict and a liar.

'I wish I'd been there for you, Becca.'

Her hand reached out again and stayed on his knee. 'Me too. We'd have done better together, I think.'

She was probably right. He'd been isolated in those last months in Brisbane. He hadn't made any close friends at university and he'd lived alone in his apartment, too shy to reach out for a flatmate or try and become involved in social events run by the faculty and student bodies.

She shifted to put the mug on the tray and the loss of her touch chilled him.

'Is this the reason you don't think you can have a relationship? Mental health isn't an impediment these days.'

Trust her to dig into the heart of the matter. 'It depends on the side effects.'

'You must be stable. They wouldn't have allowed you to go overseas if you weren't. You said it was the pneumonia and your skin condition that brought you home.' Her tone was faintly accusing.

'I haven't misled you. But you're right. I haven't told you everything.'

'There's more?'

'I was medicated for a long time for the depression. Over five years. Some side effects had a long-lasting result.'

Her unblinking gaze bored into him and he could see her acute brain ticking over. 'Side effects for depression and possibly aggravated by the medication?'

He could see her put all the clues together, a slight flush pinking her cheeks. 'You were impotent? Surely it would have rectified itself once you were stable and came off the medication. It's no reason to avoid relationships ... or are we talking two different things?'

His insides curled into a painful ball. His pale skin must be a beacon of bright colour, adding to his humiliation. 'It hasn't totally resolved at this time.'

'You mean the other day? It wasn't only that you weren't into me?'

She was killing him. 'It's ... unreliable.'

'You'd have had successful relationships since you went off medication.'

It wasn't a question and he didn't quite know how to respond. 'It takes a lot of trust to enter a physical relationship with someone when you're in my situation.'

Her fingers kneaded the fleecy fabric of his robe. 'Have you had a recent medical opinion?'

'It's largely mental. Performance anxiety.'

***

Becca swallowed down the lump in her throat. She couldn't imagine what Morgan had been through.

Sure, she hadn't had sex in close on thirteen years. But she hadn't exactly wanted it, either. Not with any of the men paraded in front of her by helpful friends and the hopeful Grace.

She'd been too absorbed with her children to be taking risks with a man she wasn't a hundred percent sure about. Experience had taught her to be cautious.

It was different for Morgan. To be a man whose sex life was relegated to only those women he could trust enough to reveal his inner demons must have had enormous impact on his emotional baggage and self-esteem. She wondered how many and then dismissed it. Not her business.

Now he'd been forced to open up to her, because of the necessity of making the co-parenting relationship work.

'Is there anything I can do to help?'

His laugh was a ragged thing that showed the rawness of his emotions. 'I don't think so.'

He'd already found her less than adequate in bed, which made it a stupid question. Stupid and embarrassing. 'Does Grace know?'

'Only about the depression and anxiety. Not the unfortunate side effects. Not a conversation I want to have with my mother.'

Yet he was having it with her. Something hopeful curled into life in her chest. 'And this is why you're never going to marry. That's what you meant, isn't it?'

'What woman would take someone who was only half a man?'

'Why do you think you're only half a man? It's a medical condition. Not an uncommon one. Besides, having sex isn't the measure of a real man.'

He tugged at his earlobe, a sign he was aware of revealing heat under his skin. 'All the same, it's not exactly a recommendation for going into a normal marriage. Most women would baulk at it.'

'The right woman wouldn't.'

His eyes were ice cold. 'You're suggesting I try out every woman of my acquaintance like some princess trying on a glass slipper to see if it fits?'

'That does sound kind of problematic. I was more thinking you could find someone who doesn't find the sex thing a concern.'

'There is only one woman I've ever wanted to marry, and she wants sex.'

Nausea caught in her throat as she tried to visualise the kind of woman he wanted. Someone who fitted his mother's vision of the perfect wife? Had he asked someone and been rejected? One of the women Grace had mentioned?

'Did you ask her if she'd be prepared to take less? It's not like you can't give her physical satisfaction, even if some things don't co-operate.'

'Would you?'

Heat was rising up her throat at the intimacy of this conversation. 'Like a shot, if I loved him.'

He was looking at her like she was some kind of creepy crawly. 'Why?'

'Marriage is not only about sex. It's about intimacy and being in the same space mentally as well as physically. There are lots of marriages where full sexual relationships aren't possible but they're still loving and fulfilling marriages.'

Now she sounded like a marriage counsellors manual.

He straightened his leg, turning to sit on the side of the bed, facing away from her. 'Would you marry a man to provide a father for your children if you knew physical intimacy might never happen?'

'That's not something I could answer without considering a lot of other things. What kind of father he'd make. Whether we could be friends. What level of intimacy he'd want.'

'Would you marry me for the sake of the children?'

All the air left the room; her chest tightening until she thought it might implode. How to react? Was he serious or was this another of those speculative scenarios?

'It could be a logical option to our situation.' It came out all breathy with a squeak that hurt her throat.

'I don't want you to take the children away. The whole idea of putting distance between us was me being a coward.'

'A coward?'

'I didn't want to have to tell you about my ... problem.'

'It must be embarrassing. Is that why you kept away in the first place? Once you were qualified?'

'I didn't know it would be ongoing at that stage. The simple truth is, I was ashamed. I fell apart at the first challenge. I didn't want to face anyone. I didn't want to face you.'

The hopeful something around her heart expanded some more. 'Why me, Morgan?'

'Because I never forgot you. After everything I thought about you, about what I believed you'd done, I missed you. We'd been friends for years. I had no-one else I could talk to in the same way, someone I trusted. There were colleagues who were friends, but I was never tempted to speak to them about my issues.'

'I missed you too. Only I wasn't alone. I had the children and they are such a part of you, it was like having you with me.'

'You've done an amazing job with them.'

'I couldn't have done it without your parents' help.'

He kind of snort laughed and she couldn't help smiling back.

'I'm serious. Grace did a great job babysitting when they were small. It meant I could finish school and do my training.'

'I still feel ... I don't know. Angry? Guilty? We'll never know what might have happened if I'd known about the children first up. I've missed a decade and more of their lives. Yet looking back, I don't know if I would have coped with the responsibility. Once I was considered cured, I still had times when stress affected my capacity to cope. For most of the time, I kept my head down, tail up, focusing on my job. Just getting by.'

'Did you enjoy your time in Africa?'

He shifted, bringing his other leg onto the bed and moving to lean on the pillows beside her. He kept his gaze on the far side of the room but his hand sought hers, twining their fingers together and resting them on his bare thigh.

'I don't know if I could say I enjoyed it. Dealing with the local people taught me a lot. When I arrived I was still in the middle of a giant pity party. Seeing the conditions they had to live with, woke me up quick smart.'

'Your mother told us you were usually based in some of the poorest areas.'

'I'd seen documentaries and we did some basic training to prepare us for the local conditions. All the same, I was shocked at the level of poverty. I always thought your family had it rough, and I still think it was tough by Australian standards, yet this was something else again.'

'Will you go back?'

'I've been advised not to. There are other things I can do to help.'

'Does that mean you'll stay permanently?'

He met her gaze, his thigh shifting to press against her leg under the fleecy robe. 'I want to stay. I'd like to marry and raise a family. Do you think it's a crazy dream?'

She'd like to think he was asking her specifically, but she'd read him wrong too many times. 'Not crazy if you work for it.'

'If I want the family to be you and Edward and Gabby, do you think that's a possibility?'

'They'd love it.'

'How about you? Would you love it?'

Her courage failed her. 'I don't know. Will there be the real kind of love involved?'

His grip on her hand tightened. 'I've loved you since forever, Becca. I suspect it's a chronic condition.'

She couldn't mistake the sincerity in the simple statement. It was there in the strain of his voice and the melting warmth of his eyes, the corners creased with anxiety.

'Morgan...' She swallowed the emotion and cleared her throat. 'I feel the same. I can't remember a time when I didn't love you.'

There was pain in the drawn lines of his face. 'What about when I accused you of all those things and then abandoned you?'

She placed her free hand on his chest, over his heart. 'I won't deny it hurt. At times the loneliness made me want to roll over and die.

At first it was anger keeping me going, getting up in the morning, going to school. Facing the gossips. Your mother played her part, once she got involved, though a negative one. I was determined to prove myself to her. I wouldn't let myself give up. No way was she going to sneer at me for not graduating or getting my certificate or holding a job.'

The words hardly left her mouth when he was hauling her into his arms, wrapping himself around her, absorbing her into his heat.

The warmth touched her heart, triggering that long-ago sensation of safety.

The scent of his freshly washed body invaded her senses, sparking a reaction in her gut, a burning of her skin where they touched. She stayed quiescent in his hold, enjoying the moment, conscious of not pressuring him with intimations of desire.

'I don't deserve you, Rebecca Walters.'

'It's not about what we deserve.'

He lifted his head to look into her eyes. 'No. You're right. For which I'm profoundly grateful.'

His hand guided her head against his throat, fingers splayed over her hair. They stayed wrapped together for what seemed like hours, her head tucked under his chin, their bodies intertwined loosely. It was deliciously comfortable.

Encroaching sleep relaxed her limbs, closing her eyes and slackening the tension in her body.

Chapter 17

Becca knew it wasn't morning, but there was a touch of light coming through the window. A luminescence that suggested there'd been more snow during the night. The children would love it. She wiggled a bit to see the time on the clock over Morgan's shoulder.

Four o'clock was too early to contact the hospital. They'd have rung if Edward had relapsed. There hadn't been a peep from her phone, sitting with its darkened screen on the bedside table alongside Morgan's.

Morgan stirred, muttering in his sleep but fell silent again as she settled back onto the pillow, conscious of her legs tangled with his. Naked legs. Somewhere during the night she'd fought her way out of the robe. She remembered it vaguely. The soft fabric of Morgan's t-shirt and boxers brushed against her bare skin. One of his arms stretched under her neck and the other curled over her waist, his large hand resting on the curve at the base of her spine.

It was more than nice. It felt like home.

Her eyes were adjusting to the faint light, allowing her to examine his face, a soft breath away from hers on the pillow. She ached to kiss him; his mouth, soft in sleep; the vulnerable, blue-veined lids of his eyes.

Not going there.

Twice she'd initiated lovemaking and twice she'd been left a fool. Understanding why he'd pulled away last time didn't give her the courage to try again.

His arm tightened, pulled her firm against his body, her pelvis locking against his as her legs tightened automatically.

'Nice.' His muttered approval came out slurred.

There was a certain hardness about him that sent her hormones clamouring. This could be simply the normal male tendency for morning erections. It probably didn't mean anything, considering his explanations of the night before. Achieving arousal was one thing. Maintaining it was the challenge.

Her own arousal was another thing entirely. The roughness of the hair on his legs chafed against the tender flesh of her inner thighs and her nipples brushed the soft fabric of his shirt, forming hard peaks. If he woke up fully, he couldn't fail to notice.

'Becca?'

It was clearer now, the deep tones offering more than a query of who shared his bed.

'Hmmm?'

'How did you sleep?'

'Best ever.'

He rubbed a cool cheek against hers. 'Me too. I could get used to this.'

There was a question in the quiet words and she snuggled closer. 'I wouldn't object.'

'Do you mean it?' He lay still under her touch, as if he held his breath, waiting.

'Do you want me to?'

'Absolutely.' His fingers dug into her hips and she flinched. 'Sorry.'

His warm hand soothed the bruised flesh, lighting small flames under the skin. They radiated out in ever increasing circles that stung and burned the closer his hand came to the base of her spine, gliding lower to where her thighs parted.

A gasp escaped as he delved deep and a shudder swept through her.

'Becca? Let me love you.'

She could barely formulate the words of assent. 'Yes.' He released her immediately, rolling away to switch on the lamp and climb out of bed, picking up his phone. He scrolled through the messages and with a satisfied nod, put it back on the bedside table.

'Is something wrong?'

'No.' He grinned at her. 'Nothing at all.'

She watched him peel off his t-shirt and then hesitate at the waistband of his boxers. In the dim light of the lamp, she recognised the struggle and waited for him to decide if he could trust her. When he dropped his briefs, she had to swallow the lump in her throat, forcing herself to focus on him. His body was beautiful, still thin after his illness but perfectly proportioned. Partially aroused, but she wasn't going to focus on what might be happening.

'How did you get so built?'

The colour dipped and swayed over his throat. 'I did a lot of exercise as part of my regime to get fit. Once I was stable I could be weaned off the medication. My doctor suggested it and it helped. I've kept it going over the years for a whole range of reasons.'

'I only do the bike riding. And gardening.'

'You look amazing.'

He sounded like he meant it, a kind of awe in his voice.

He fiddled with the bedcovers, tugging at the quilt. 'Are you warm enough?'

It was cooler at this early hour, but the heaters were still doing their job. There was a slight chill in the air where her shoulders were exposed. 'It's fresh but not unpleasant.'

He crawled back into the bed and tentatively touched her arm. 'Is my hand cold?'

'Not at all.'

'You're okay with me doing this?'

'I can sign a document if you want.'

He smiled again, recognising the teasing note. 'I like to be sure before I start an operation.'

'What are we operating on today?'

His brow creased as if he weren't as confident as he was trying to appear. 'I want to make you feel good.'

'Go ahead. Make my day.'

His face creased in a grin, as if he remembered the old movies they'd watched together, long before they matured enough to see each other in a romantic light. He stroked her shoulder with gentle fingers which seared the skin all the same.

'I plan to.'

She shivered at his touch, loving the slow sweep of his hand over her body. He moved to lie hard against her side, half propped up so he could watch her face as his fingers traced her breasts, circling her nipples until they puckered into hard nubs. As his hand crept lower, tangling in the soft curls below her stomach, she couldn't stay passive any longer.

Reaching up she hooked her arms around his neck, bringing him down until his breath caressed her cheek and mouth, warming them in the cool air. He resisted for a moment and she lifted her head, seeking his mouth. At the same moment he delved deep, finding the slickness indicating her readiness.

She bucked against his hand, unprepared for the suddenness of her body's response. His tongue licked at her mouth, tasting her and echoing the motion of his hand, her pelvis picking up the rhythm. Tension built, winding itself around her, sizzling along the pathways of her nerves. Her whole body pulsed with the surges of feeling that came from the touch of his mouth and hands. He lifted her upper body with his other arm and his chest chafed against her nipples, sending darts of something almost painful ricocheting around her insides and joining the throbbing ache at her centre.

His heart pounded strong and fast against her breast, matching the rhythm inside her as she soared higher and higher, only to melt in the flames of an explosion that rocked her to the core.

His arms held her tight as she came down, shuddering as her body sent out aftershocks.

She could happily live with this.

They lay still after she'd stopped twitching, their breathing slowing. Becca wondered how involved he'd been, if his breathing and heartrate matched hers. It must mean a similar state of arousal. With a gentle shove, she put him on his back, allowing her to slither onto his body, both of them clammy with a film of perspiration.

His penis pressed hard against her hip, damp with the same liquid heat that burned in her own body.

His hands came to rest on her waist, a slight tremor echoing her own. Tilting her head, she met the vivid blue of his eyes, faintly apprehensive if the crease between his brows were any indication.

'My turn.' She licked his throat, tasting the tang of his body. It had been too long to recall how he'd tasted as a nineteen-year-old. All excitement and nerves back then. Maybe it was the same.

She focused on his mouth, nipping and tasting until he returned the favour, kissing her back with the same intensity of the young man she'd loved all those years ago. His hands roamed over her back and she kept her own hands moving, learning his body in its new form, shaping the muscle of his shoulders, down over his pectorals until he quivered at the touch of her fingers.

A swift shift of her pelvis centred her over his body and she guided him in, feeling the stretch as he filled her.

His shocked exclamation broke the kiss and she reared up to see his expression.

The lamp cast a soft light over his face, sparking the blue of his eyes among the shadows of his sharp bones and sensitive hollows. She tightened her interior muscles and a response echoed her movement, a twitch that spiralled into sensation deep inside.

His gaze never left hers as she rocked on his pelvis, working into a rhythm that sent a flood of red from his chest and higher, to paint dark strips of colour across his cheekbones. Her body ached for more but she didn't dare break the spell keeping Morgan under her, his skin dewing with the heat building between them. His hips rotated under hers to join the pattern of movement, pushing him further and deeper.

So close. So close.

A jagged ripple rocked his body from top to toe, almost unseating her but his strong fingers gripped her thighs, keeping her in place as he cried out his release, the flash of heat taking her almost to the peak but falling away too soon.

She recognised the moment he realised he'd left her hanging and his hand moved but she pushed it away. 'It's okay. It's fine.'

She flopped onto his body and he wrapped his arms around her, rolling them onto their sides, still connected.

'I'm sorry, Becca.'

She pushed damp hair back from his forehead. 'I'm good. Really.'

His hold tightened and he buried his face in her throat, his body racked with emotion.

Her eyes filled with tears when she recognised the muffled sobs that signified the intensity of his reaction. He'd trusted her and found his own trust in himself. It was much more than she could ever hope for. Whatever happened now, she would treasure this night.

***

Morgan stared over the snow-covered fields, trying to recapture the moment of despair when he'd thought he'd lost all hope of a future with Becca and his children.

He couldn't. He was chock full of emotions; his head spinning, but despair was not one of them.

Becca lay replete in his bed, snuggled under the quilt. He'd made up for his earlier deficiency with an almost embarrassing enthusiasm. Like a teenager discovering sex for the first time. Becca hadn't exactly discouraged him and they'd enjoyed a blissful romp before falling into sleep once more. At least Becca slept. He'd been too full of unruly sensations to sleep.

Warm hands slid around his waist and clasped themselves at his midriff. She rested her head against his back, her warmth melding against his naked flesh. 'Couldn't you sleep?'

'I rang the hospital. Edward slept like a lamb and is wallowing in the attention. I said we'd be there around nine.'

Becca pulled away, allowing him to turn around. 'That'll give me time to go home and change.'

A frown wrinkled her brow as she pulled on his robe and went out to the sunroom to collect her clothes. Had they resolved things, or only added a layer of complicated to the situation?

He pulled on fresh underwear, almost regretting the shower, washing away Becca's scent from his body. Jeans and a long-sleeved t-shirt were a good start. He'd have to use a jumper and his bomber jacket this morning, the ski jacket still needing salvaging after its drenching.

Becca didn't give him a chance to ask questions, scurrying out of the bathroom in her clothes from last night. 'Can you give me a lift or will I walk?'

'I'll drive you. It'll save time and we can head straight into the hospital.'

She was checking her messages in the car and flung herself out the moment they arrived at her place. 'I'll be as quick as I can.'

He sat in the car for a moment, watching her half jog around the back of the house.

This wasn't going to work. They had to have things clear before they picked up Edward.

The house was cold from being left empty overnight. He flicked on the heater in the kitchen and the children's bedroom before heading to Becca's room.

She was gathering her clothes together and frowned as he entered the room. 'I said I'd be as quick as I can. I need a shower.'

'I'll come and talk to you while you wash then.' She opened her mouth to protest but he held up his hand. 'We have to have things sorted between us before we see Edward. I thought we had, but you've been avoiding talking.'

She stalked past him to the bathroom and turned on the heater and exhaust fan. 'I don't know what to say. Things are different this morning.'

A tightness sat high in his chest at her retreat. 'Why are they different? I thought we agreed we loved each other and we could look at marriage and creating a family.'

She hesitated as she pulled her boots off. 'The situation isn't quite the same. You have more possibilities.'

'As far as I know, you are the only person who is the mother of my children and the only person I love.'

Avoiding his eyes, she adjusted the shower over the bathtub. 'You have more options now. You don't have to worry about the ... the sex thing.'

She peeled off her clothes and quickly stepped into the old claw-footed tub and pulled the curtain, obscuring her from his sight.

'The sex thing?'

He pulled the curtain back and she gasped a protest, turning her back on him.

'Becca, I've seen it all and touched most of it. I can manage to look at your face when I'm talking to you and considering the importance of what we're talking about, I think face to face is necessary.'

Water ran down her body and he acknowledged it wasn't quite as easy to ignore as he'd made out. Fortunately for his sanity, she'd turned back around, sluicing the water over her head ready to wash it and he was able to fix his gaze on her face.

'First of all, what makes you think I don't have to worry about the sex thing?'

Her hair was a mass of white froth as she scrubbed it. 'You know you can, you know, do it. That should give you confidence in other situations.'

He leaned against the wall beside the head of the bath. 'Are you suggesting I should go and do the whole princess thing to test your theory?'

'No.' She spluttered as soap went into her eyes and mouth and he reached up and redirected the shower head.

'You're forgetting the key ingredient. Trust. There aren't too many women in the world I trust enough to risk making a fool of myself in bed.'

Becca switched off the shower and buried her face in a towel. 'Who are these other women?'

'No-one that need concern you. I don't risk relationships with colleagues on principle.'

'Why would you trust me? You didn't when it came to Dan.'

Morgan shifted so she wasn't directly in his line of sight while she dried herself. 'I've thought a lot about my feelings back then. Before I knew the truth, I realised the anger was misdirected. Once I was older and my headspace cleared, I realised I was holding a sixteen-year-old to a standard many adults struggle with. My anger was more about losing your friendship. I blamed you for not being my friend far more than for being with Dan. I needed you and you weren't there.

When I was coming home, I think I subconsciously hoped to reconnect. Believing you were with Dan activated all the resentment again. I'm sorry.'

'You believed it easily. Both times.'

'You aren't the only person who wonders if they're good enough. I've disappointed my parents, my teachers and my girlfriend. You, in case you were wondering. Dan had an advantage I didn't have. He was in your life all the time. I was away at university and I spent far too much time worrying about whether you'd give up on me because I was never there.'

Becca stood wide eyed; the towel draped down her front. 'You should have known it was never going to happen. I'd been crushing on you forever and if the other boys were interested, I certainly wasn't. Dan ... well you understand about him now, I hope.'

'Is it still about the teenage crush?'

'No. I love grown-up Morgan more.'

He blinked away the emotion and held out a hand. 'You've turned into an amazing woman, Becca Walters.'

With a soft gasp, she flung herself at him, rocking him back on his heels. Holding her tight he tilted her chin up. 'Rebecca Walters. You're the only woman I've ever loved. Will you marry me and make us a family?'

'Yes. Yes. Forever and eternity.'

Epilogue

Becca smoothed down the fabric of her dress as she stood at the door of the church. Grace had demonstrated her commitment to this marriage by bringing out the wedding dress worn by the Maiden girl who'd married a Cavanaugh after the First World War.

It was a lovely thing with a three-quarter length silk slip, silk chiffon overlay with long sleeves trimmed with fine lace and tiny knots of ribbon at the collar and cuffs. It had once been white, but the years had turned it into a pale milk coffee colour which suited Becca far more than stark white would have done.

The veil had long been lost, but Thackery twisted her a crown of spring flowers arranged to sit high on her forehead and trailed a length of coffee-coloured satin ribbon from the bow at the back.

Her make-up was immaculate for the era, understated but enhancing her eyes and making her lips lush and inviting, courtesy of Marcia Kavocik who had a vast knowledge of vintage make-up styles. Thackery and Win organised it as a surprise and Becca was grateful. Marcia was lovely, helping her overcome the dread of making a fool of herself in front of half the town.

Keeping a low profile had become second nature over the years, which made being the centre of attention at a wedding kind of her worst nightmare.

Thackery somehow found top hat and tails with an ivory shirt and cravat for the ceremony where he was giving her away. His hair was up in a bun and hidden by the hat, though he wouldn't be able to keep it on in the church. Along with Morgan's matching gear, it would look fabulous in the wedding photos.

Edward was in a similar outfit, without the jacket and hat at his request, a waistcoat dressing up the ivory shirt and trousers. Gabby was in her element, a frilly dress in an apricot that didn't clash as much with her hair as her favourite shade of pink.

Win, looking like a feminine version of her brother, handed her a bouquet, fragrant with herbs and delicate flowers to match the wreath on her hair and slipped into the church.

It was time to do the bride thing.

The twins made their entrance first, walking side by side, pacing to the entrance music. Grace had insisted on the full deal. Once she'd capitulated, she'd been all in, as if once she was no longer afraid of breaking, she realised she could bend. Which she did with a grace befitting her name.

Becca spotted Morgan instantly, his height and bright hair drawing her gaze, the much shorter Michael Long standing as his best man. She was halfway down the aisle before Morgan turned and she almost stumbled at the passion blazing in those blue eyes. The rest of the congregation faded to nothing as she homed in on the man she'd loved for most of her life. It was unbelievable that after all these years, the small, impossible dreams she'd nurtured as a teenager had come to fruition.

The ceremony was a blur, but she must have remembered the words because no-one had to prompt her. Finally, they reached the part where they kissed and her body woke up as his mouth teased hers. It was as natural as breathing to cling, tasting him, taking in the familiar scent of him. She blinked as he drew away and turned her to face the congregation.

Grace was unashamedly teary and Laureen gave Becca an irreverent thumbs up from her seat to one side. She sucked in an unsteady breath. She'd given herself away in front of half the town and suddenly it didn't matter a bit. She had nothing to be ashamed of. Twining her fingers with Morgan's long elegant ones, she beamed over the crowd, unable to stop herself from smiling.

Morgan tightened his grip, the intimacy of palm to palm contact sending a frisson like pure alcohol through her veins. A flush of pink blossomed at his throat and she revelled in the knowledge he was as much affected by her touch as she was by his.

By the time they were seated at the reception, photos taken, congratulations received, speeches over and toasts drunk, Becca was exhausted but riding on a high. The twins were running wild, glad to be released from the formal part of the evening. The only thing left was the cake cutting which Marcia was organising with her usual efficiency.

Morgan murmured in her ear, sending a shiver down her spine. 'Happy, Mrs. Cavanaugh?'

Becca stilled. 'Oh lord, I never thought of that.'

'What do you mean?' Morgan smiled tenderly down at her, one arm draped over the back of her seat.

She leaned into him. 'Once upon a time my biggest fear was becoming your mother.'

They both glanced over at his parents who seemed to have achieved some kind of deeper understanding in the aftermath of Edward's accident. Grace would never relinquish her public persona, but in private she was definitely softer. Affectionate with the twins and while Becca's own relationship with her mother-in-law was still in a growing stage, she could consider her a friend at last.

Morgan tightened his grip on her shoulder, the other hand coming to rest low on her abdomen. 'We're both going to be in her bad books once we tell her our news.'

Becca placed her hand over his, warmth flooding her chest. 'She won't be able to deny she's a grandmother this time.'

They watched as Gabby came up behind the older couple and draped her arms over them both. Morgan laughed as Grace flushed with pleasure. 'I don't think it will be such a problem. The twins are breaking her into being a "proper grandma" with their usual determination.'

Becca hesitated and then forced out the words. 'Are you happy about the baby? We never discussed having more children.'

He tilted up her chin and kissed her gently. 'I'm thrilled. This time I get to experience the whole shebang. It's the one thing I regret about the twins—missing those years.'

'I won't be able to work full-time for a while after the birth.'

'By then, we'll have plenty of staff in place to take up the slack.'

At this moment, she wasn't overly worried. Things were working out at the clinic, the two of them working together as a team. That was the best thing of all, the way they were in tune, sharing a vision for the future.

A sensation of warmth permeated her whole body. It seemed like, after all these years, they could and would have it all.

***

'Sorry to disturb the lovebirds, but it's time to cut the cake.'

Morgan tried not to curse as Marcia interrupted the moment.

They followed her to one side of the room where the cake was set up. It was a fabulous concoction made entirely of cupcakes on a stand Win had painted in white and gold to match the white icing with gold fondant ornaments on the top of each cake. Edward and Gabby were already beside the table, rather smug about the spectacular result of their planning. His mother had wanted a more traditional iced fruit cake, but the twins overruled her.

Marcia handed them the knife, indicating the larger than usual cupcake in the centre of the display and the crowd hushed, glasses of champagne sitting idle.

The knife sliced cleanly through the cake and the guests applauded.

Gabby bounced up and down. 'You touched the bottom, that means you have to kiss the nearest boy, Mum.'

Morgan laughed as Becca's skin took on a rosy hue. 'If those are the rules.'

The tinkle of cutlery against crystal filled the room and Morgan turned Becca to face him. The love in her eyes was everything he craved. It made the struggles of the last thirteen years worthwhile.

It hadn't been easy, but perhaps they were stronger people for it. Better able to make this marriage a success. He did have everything a man could want. His children, family, most of all, the woman he loved more than life.

Her fingers twined into his hair, her smile mischievous. 'Don't keep us waiting, my love.'

Morgan relaxed into her hold, meeting her lips with the same eagerness she displayed. He melted into her kiss, the feeling of coming home irradiating the moment.

Yes. He had everything.

Thanks for reading *A Matter of Trust*. I hope you enjoyed it.

Sign up to our **newsletter** and find out about new releases, must-read series and **ebook deals** at romance.com.au.

Reviews can help readers find books, and I am grateful for all honest reviews. Thank you for taking the time to let others know what you've read, and what you thought.

Share your reading experience on:
Facebook
Instagram
romance.com.au